Fourth Grade
Fairy

GNOME INVASION

Fourth Grade Fairy

GNOME INVASION

Eileen Cook

Aladdin

New York London Toronto Sydney

ALADDIN

An imprint of Simon & Schuster Children's Publishing Division
1230 Avenue of the Americas, New York, NY 10020
First Aladdin paperback edition August 2011
Copyright © 2011 by Eileen Cook
All rights reserved, including the right of reproduction in whole or in part in any form.
ALADDIN is a trademark of Simon & Schuster, Inc., and related logo is a registered
trademark of Simon & Schuster, Inc.
For information about special discounts for bulk purchases, please contact
Simon & Schuster Special Sales at 1-866-506-1949 or business@simonandschuster.com.
The Simon & Schuster Speakers Bureau can bring authors to your live event.
For more information or to book an event contact the
Simon & Schuster Speakers Bureau at 1-866-248-3049 or visit our website
at www.simonspeakers.com.
Designed by Karina Granda
The text of this book was set in Lomba.
Manufactured in the United States of America 0711 OFF
2 4 6 8 10 9 7 5 3 1
Library of Congress Control Number 2011930732
ISBN 978-1-4169-9813-6
ISBN 978-1-4169-9816-7 (eBook)

one

Being able to shrink down and fly:
   a. is way more fun than you might have thought it would be
   b. really ticks off your know-it-all older sister because she thought it was her special ability
   c. comes in handy, especially if you want to spy on your sister
   d. all of the above

It's a fact well-known by little sisters everywhere, that if you sister doesn't want you around, it is because she is either a) doing something really cool and thinks you'll ruin it, or b) doing something she shouldn't. My sister, Lucinda, had made this big deal about how she couldn't be disturbed because she was working on a school project, but it didn't seem to me that homework was her focus. She just didn't want me around.

My sister had invited over Evan, who was a year ahead of her in school, to help with a project. Of course it wasn't any type of normal school project. My family are fairies, fairy godmothers to be exact. I didn't always fit in because I'm more interested in humdrums—aka humans—than magic. I'd even convinced my parents to send me to Riverside Elementary School where I made a humdrum best friend. I might not be as interested in magic as my sister, but even I knew Lucinda wasn't that interested in getting an A in her potions class. Evan might be good with potions, but I was pretty sure the real reason my sister wanted him to come over was because he was the cutest fairy at Cottingley Fairy Academy. He had dark curly hair that always seemed just a little too long, so he always had to push it out of his eyes. He had this way of smiling where his mouth curved up on one side and his left eye closed a bit like he was winking at you. As soon as he arrived, Lucinda had dragged him into the living room and made my mom promise that Katie and I wouldn't be allowed in because they had to work to do.

This was totally unfair because you could tell that

Evan wanted to talk to Katie and me. Almost everyone in the fairy community was fascinated to find out I had a real, live, humdrum friend. For centuries fairies have lived secretly among humdrums. I was supposed to keep the fact I was a fairy a secret in my humdrum school, but my friend Katie had figured it out. Katie wants to be a detective. And an astronaut. And to win an Olympic gold medal for gymnastics. My best friend is very talented.

She's also nosy. Katie had noticed there were a lot of things about my family and me that didn't make sense. Like the fact I had conversations with my dog. Of course she could only hear my side, but Winston and I had full conversations, although sometimes he did a lot more talking at me than with me. She thought we might be spies, but when she found out the truth about us being magical she decided that was even cooler. Some fairies were worried that humdrums wouldn't be able to cope with knowing that fairies really existed, but Katie jumped right in and helped me grant my first wish. She wasn't even freaked out by the Tooth Fairy, and trust me, a tooth fairy can be a bit intimidating.

There was something else special about having Katie as a best friend. Once Katie knew that I was a fairy, things started to change. I started to change. My grandma thought it had something to do with having humdrums believe in magic again. She thought maybe we need someone to believe in us in order to keep our magical abilities strong. Fairies can do all kinds of magic spells, but we each have only one special magic talent. Mine is talking to animals, which—I don't want to brag or anything, but—is pretty cool.

The weird thing was that once Katie knew I was a fairy I got a second magical ability. I could fly. To be technical about it, I floated first, and I didn't have any control over it. It just happened—and in the middle of a humdrum wedding, too. I quickly learned how to control it, because shrinking down to the size of a bug and flying around like a giant bumblebee isn't something you want to do willy-nilly. If I wanted to fly all I had to do was concentrate on the idea and think light thoughts. It felt funny, sort of tingly, but shrinking down didn't hurt, and being able to stretch out the tiny wings hidden under my shoulder blades felt great. (If you don't stretch them every so often they can cramp.) I couldn't keep the fact that I was flying secret from my parents. They might not have realized I was floating as long as I stayed pretty close to the ground, but when I started shrinking down like a sparkling, glowing firefly they were bound to notice.

Once my parents knew I could fly, they wanted to know how I came to be the first fairy who had two magical powers. I had to tell them about Katie. This past week my parents and grandma had been going to meetings with the Fairy Council. Everyone was trying to figure out what it meant that our secret was out. There was now a humdrum who knew there were fairies. My sister didn't spend her time worrying about how our whole society might change. She spent the past week talking about how it wasn't fair that I could fly since that was her thing. (As if she invented flying!) I spent my week trying to figure out the tricks of flying, like how to keep from bumping into the walls. Once I sneezed midflight and shot all the way across the room like a rocket. Turns out flying is more complicated than it looks.

So even though my sister said Evan came by to help with her homework, I knew it was likely he came to see Katie and me. After all, knowing a humdrum is a pretty big deal. My mom caught us staring out through the railing of the staircase into the living room trying to get a view of Evan. She shooed us back to my room, saying

EILEEN COOK

they needed their privacy. I tried pointing out that we weren't in the living room, or bothering them, but she still made us leave.

Katie flopped across my bed, nearly landing on my dog, Winston, who had been sleeping under the covers. "I want to visit the Fairy Academy if there are boys who look like that!"

"You should see Evan play draolo. He's amazing," I said.

"What's that?" Katie asked, sitting up and scratching Winston's ears.

"Draolo. It's like polo only with dragons." Katie's eyes grew wide, so I went on to explain so she wouldn't have the wrong idea. "They're not *huge* dragons or anything. They're raised for the game, sort of horse-size, but they can snort fire and fly."

"That is so cool. I would love to own a pet dragon," Katie said.

Winston rolled over so Katie could rub his belly. "Pfft, why would anyone want a dragon as a pet when they could have a dog?" he asked. "Dogs are superior creatures in almost every way."

Since I was the one who could communicate with animals I had to translate for Katie. "Winston thinks you're better off with a dog. He's a bit of a dog snob, but he is right about this. Dragons are okay, but they aren't housebroken and they can be kind of smelly," I warned Katie.

"Still, it's a dragon. I bet Evan looks really cute riding one." Katie sighed, and then perked up. "Maybe we should make up a plate of your mom's cookies and bring them to Evan and your sister. Doing homework can make someone pretty hungry. Giving people food isn't bugging them, it's being polite."

"It is polite, but my sister will freak out and say we're doing it just to spy on her," I explained. Katie looked annoyed. I had tried to tell her before how lucky she was to be an only child. Now she was starting to understand what a pain older sisters could be.

"Do you think Evan likes your sister?"

I scrunched up my eyebrows while I thought about it. It was possible. I wasn't exactly an expert on boys. Everyone kept telling me that Nathan Filler in my class liked me because he would tease me and throw the fries from his hot lunch at me. It didn't make sense to me, but humdrum boys are complicated. My sister, despite her many flaws, *was* pretty. Plus, she tended to keep her really evil behavior directed at me. She was usually quite nice to other people. "He might like her. He doesn't have to help with her potion homework. He must be doing it for a reason."

"I wonder what they're talking about?" Katie asked.

"I bet they're talking about us," I said. "It's a really big deal to other fairies that we're friends."

"Don't you want to know what he thinks? We could send Winston down to listen to their conversation and then come back and tell us what he said," Katie suggested.

"I beg your pardon! I have no intention of getting involved in some sort of boy-crazy spy mission." Winston rolled over so he could stand.

"We could give him some bologna to make it worth his time." Katie might not be able to understand Winston the same way that I did, but she was a pretty good at knowing what made him tick.

Winston's head cocked over to the side. "Bologna? Now, maybe I was being a bit hasty when I said I wouldn't do it. I would consider simply strolling downstairs, and if I happened to overhear a discussion, there certainly isn't anything sneaky about sharing the details." Winston's tongue fell out of his mouth as he started thinking about a giant mound of bologna slices.

"Easy, my canine James Bond." I turned to Katie. "This plan won't work. Lucinda knows I can communicate with Winston. No way she would let him wander into the room, plop down, and listen. She'd kick him out of the living room so fast all we would see would be a furry black blur."

The three of us were silent while we tried to think of a plan that would work.

"You could still get me some bologna. I think better with processed meat snacks." Winston turned in a circle to mat the bedspread into a comfy pile and then flopped down with his head on his paws.

"What I wouldn't give to be a fly on the wall," Katie said.

Katie and I both looked over at each other at the same second and squealed. It was a perfect plan.

two

True or False:

If you want to see or hear the really interesting stuff, sometimes you have to be willing to spy.

Answer:

True! Especially if you want to see your sister kiss a boy. Not that you want to actually see *that*, but you are interested in things like, how do you know who tilts their head left and who tilts right, not to mention if you should close your eyes or not. How are you supposed to know how to kiss someone when the time comes if you don't do some investigation?

BONUS QUESTION:

True or False:
   Your parents will totally understand that the spying was done in the name of scientific investigation.

Answer:
   False, with a capital F.

You know the tingle you get in your nose just a second before you sneeze? That's what it feels like to shrink down to firefly-size, only instead of in your nose it feels that way all over your body. There was a *POP* sound and suddenly I was hovering just above Katie's head. I stretched my wings out and gave them a good shake.

   "I think this is the coolest thing ever," Katie said. "Did you know you have sort of a green sparkle? It's a nice green too, kinda apple-colored."

   I nodded, but I wasn't sure if she could tell I was agreeing with her. This was one of the problems with being this small. The other problem was that if I flew in front of an air conditioner I could get sucked into the vent. My sister had almost gotten eaten by a lizard once, but I think that was partly her own fault.

Katie opened my bedroom door and I fluttered out into the hallway. I wanted to show off a little, so I put on a burst of speed as I flew down the stairs. I was going so fast I smacked into the back of my dad who was walking into the kitchen. I hadn't expected anyone to be in the hall. I guess this is why there are recommended in-house flying speed limits. I clung to Dad's tweed jacket and shook my head to clear it. He turned around to see who tapped him on the shoulder, but of course the hallway was empty. I held my breath and tried to keep my wings as still as possible so that he wouldn't realize I was there. If my dad caught me now, the spying mission would be over before I even got a peek at Evan and Lucinda.

I waited until my dad turned back to go into the kitchen and then I flew off. I bopped along the hallway until I reached the doorway to the living room. I peeked around. Evan and Lucinda were sitting on the sofa.

Lucinda shut her potions book with a huff. "I swear I'll never get the hang of those transformation spells."

"Don't be hard on yourself, they're tricky." Evan put

his hand down next to hers on the sofa so that they were almost touching.

"You never make it look hard," Lucinda said. She looked at Evan and then giggled. She must have been nervous, because her giggle turned into a snort. I could see her flush bright red. Evan was such a gentleman that he didn't mention that my sister was a pig snorter. That's how I could tell he was a quality guy.

"Here, let me show you a trick with that last potion." Evan pointed to something in his book, and my sister leaned closer to him so she could see the page.

Lucinda was concentrating on the potion, but Evan was looking at her. "You've got some hair in your eyes." Evan softly brushed the curl off her face. Lucinda gave another one of her pig snort laughs and blushed. Evan leaned closer and closed his eyes, and Lucinda closed hers as well and pooched her lips way out. Oh my gosh! They were going to kiss! *Ew!*

I flew in so I could see the lip action up close. I knew Katie was going to want all the details, like did their noses touch and did their lips make a squooshy sound. I hovered over Evan's head. His and Lucinda's lips were just about to touch when she opened her eyes. As soon as Lucinda saw me her eyes got really wide and she jerked away from Evan. She jumped up and grabbed one of the glass lab beakers they were using to mix potions off the coffee table.

I tried to fly backward as fast as I could, but when my sister is angry she can move really quickly. Lucinda leaped over the sofa. Evan nearly fell off, he was so shocked. Lucinda slammed the glass beaker against the living room wall, trapping me inside. She slid her hand over the top of the beaker and peered in. Her eye looked huge from in there. I beat my hands against the glass wall and yelled for her to let me go. She shook the beaker.

"You are in huge trouble!" Lucinda gave the beaker another shake and I felt one of my wings bruise when it hit the glass. I was starting to feel a bit nauseated from all the shaking. "Mom! Dad!" Lucinda yelled for them as if, instead of peeking to see what she was doing, I had been sneaking up on her and Ethan with an axe.

As soon as my parents came into the room, Lucinda thrust the beaker at them. "Willow was spying on me!"

I tried to explain what was happening, but I could tell all they could hear was a buzzing sound.

My dad took the beaker from Lucinda and left the top open so that I could fly out.

POP!

I stumbled and nearly fell. I was dizzy from being bounced around. Evan was still sitting on the sofa with his mouth hanging open. He was getting a chance to see the other side of Lucinda. She was complaining loudly to our parents about how she had no privacy, and how having me as a sister was the worst thing that ever happened to her. Either she had forgotten about the time she was almost eaten by a lizard, or she thought having me as a sister was worse than being snacked on by a reptile.

"Katie and I just wanted to see what potions they were working on. If I had known they were kissing I wouldn't have bothered them," I explained.

Lucinda's head looked like it was about to explode. Evan stood up and wiped his hands on his pant legs, looking nervous.

My dad called Katie down from my room so he could talk to both of us.

Winston trailed behind Katie and looked around the room. He backed up when he saw how angry Lucinda was. "I think it would have been easier if you had simply given me the bologna," he said.

"You girls sit on the sofa," Mom pointed with her finger. "Lucinda, why don't you take Evan out to the kitchen and get a snack while we talk to your sister. We'll talk to you about rules for guests after Evan's gone home."

"I hope they sell you both for slave labor in a pixie dust mine," Lucinda said, nearly crying. She knew she was in trouble. She was spitting a bit when she spoke. That's how I knew she was really mad. That and the fact the vein in her forehead was throbbing. Like it was my fault that my parents had a no-making-out-in-the-house rule.

Evan touched her arm. "Don't be mad. I think it's cute she wants to show her humdrum friend some magic." Evan looked at Katie with his half smile. "You don't mind being called a humdrum do you?"

Katie melted. "I don't mind at all. You can call me anything you want."

"I think it is so cool that a humdrum knows we exist. This is going to change everything. You are so lucky to be a part of all of this," Evan said to Lucinda.

Lucinda was trying to look like she felt lucky, but it looked more like she wanted to throw up. She was starting to get used to the idea of Katie being at the house, but I knew being that close to a humdrum still freaked her out. She also freaks out if she sees a worm or a spider or a mouse (or hamster or gerbil—she can't tell them apart). My sister is very high-strung.

"There is some chocolate cake in the kitchen. You two help yourselves." Mom motioned again for Evan and Lucinda to leave the room.

"I was never allowed to fly around the house spying on whomever I wanted to," Lucinda pointed out as she walked toward the door. "If I had done this I would have been grounded. Willow gets away with everything."

"It's harder for me. I have to learn how to manage two powers, not just one like you," I explained. I could tell from the way my sister's eyes narrowed down that she didn't feel sorry for me. She took Evan's arm and stomped out of the room.

Mom shook her head sadly. "Girls, I've very disappointed in both of you. You know that you aren't supposed to use magic simply for fun, and certainly not for spying on Lucinda."

"I'm really sorry, Mr. and Mrs. Doyle. Spying on Lucinda was partly my idea." Katie said, looking at her lap. "Are you going to call my parents?"

"I'm not sure how we could explain this type of situation to your mom and dad," my mom said. Katie was the only human who knew we were fairies. Her parents thought I was just your average fourth grader.

I crossed my arms and slumped into the sofa. "I

know we shouldn't have spied on Lucinda, but she used to fly when she wasn't supposed to all the time. Remember what happened with the lizard Godzilla?"

"Your sister isn't perfect," my mom said. I felt like pointing out that was an understatement. "However, your sister isn't the one we're talking about here. I know this is an exciting time for the two of you, but that doesn't give you permission to do magic whenever you like. Willow, you know how nervous the Fairy Council is about having Katie know we exist and about our abilities."

"It's not like I was doing any new magic. Katie already knows I can fly," I said.

"And I won't tell anyone, I promise," Katie said. "Not about the flying, or how she can talk to Winston, or anything."

Mom smiled at Katie. "I know you won't, but you have to understand we're talking about hundreds of years of being in hiding. This is a big change for us. Fairies are going to need time to get used to this idea."

"I just wish the council would make up their minds about what to do," I said. Ever since my grandma had told the council about how Katie had figured us out, it seemed like there had been a thousand meetings. Grandma and I had to tell our stories over and over about how Katie had discovered the truth. I could tell the council had a hard time believing that Katie would hide in a tree to spy on me. That's because they don't know her very well. She knew something strange was going on and she was determined to figure it out. You don't get to be an astronaut without being really determined. We wouldn't even have known that she saw us doing magic, but gravity caught up to her and she ended up falling out of the tree. Now we needed the Fairy Council to make a decision, but I could tell that wouldn't happen quickly. The council had meetings to schedule more in-depth meetings. They had groups studying all the different options, and each of those groups had to set more meetings so they could decide how they wanted to study their particular option. Then they had meetings to make fancy presentations about what they studied. All the talk of meetings made my head spin.

"Part of the council making up their minds is the surprise inspection they're planning," my mom said. "Can you imagine if they had done that today? How would it look if they had shown up and you and Katie were using your magic to spy on your sister?"

I slouched down further in the sofa. The last thing I wanted to do was give the Fairy Council any reason to think it was a bad idea for me to have a humdrum as a best friend. "I'm sorry," I whispered.

"The people you owe an apology to are your sister and Evan."

I sighed. I should have known they would make me apologize to her. I noticed my dad was scribbling in his notebook and watching Katie very carefully.

"What sort of punishment would your parents give you if this had happened at your house?" Dad asked Katie. There was nothing my dad liked better than studying humdrum habits up close. Every time Katie came to the house he was always making notes about what she ate, what types of games she liked to play, what kind of socks she liked to wear, and her opinions on everything from TV shows to books.

"I've never really been in trouble for flying," Katie pointed out to my dad.

Dad's face fell. "Oh right, of course."

"If I've done something *really* bad, one of my parents' favorite things to do is to ask me what I think the punishment should be. I almost always pick something worse than what they would come up with on their own."

Dad's eyes lit up. "Very clever!" He scribbled it down in his notebook.

I scowled at Katie. My parents didn't need any suggestions in the punishment ideas department. "Maybe we should have to walk Winston as a punishment," I said hopefully.

Mom ruffled my hair. "Nice try. I think instead you two girls can help by cleaning out the garage and sorting the recycling."

"The whole garage?" I sighed. Our garage was enchanted so from the outside it looked normal, but inside it was huge. Plus there were a lot of creepy spiders. I'm not afraid of spiders like my sister, but that doesn't mean I want them touching me or falling into my hair.

"And don't forget to apologize to your sister," Mom added.

I sighed. Having a best friend who is a humdrum is pretty cool, and being able to fly and talk to animals is a lot of fun, but at the end of the day it is still really hard to be ten years old. Especially if you have Lucinda as a sister.

three

Space:

    a. is dark.

    b. is cold.

    c. has no good restaurants; most of your food comes dehydrated or in pouches.

    d. makes it really hard to go the bathroom.

    e. is not a place I would want to visit, but some people apparently can't wait to go.

Answer:

    F, all the above.

I glanced at the clock and tried to figure out how many seconds before the bell would ring for lunch. I was hungry and my stomach kept making loud growling noises. It sounded like I had a cougar trapped inside. My stomach was so loud that Tyler, who sat in front of me, turned around twice. I didn't meet his eyes and instead looked around as if I were trying to figure out where the sound was coming from too.

The bell rang and I leaped up from my seat. Finally!

"Before you all dash off for lunch, I have an announcement," our teacher, Ms. Caul, said. Everyone stopped in place. I hoped it wasn't a long announcement. There were cookies in my lunch sack and I was starting to get close to a cookie emergency.

"I trust everyone has been working hard on their projects for the science fair?" We were supposed to have been working on our projects for the past two weeks, but I knew some people hadn't even started yet. "I've heard some exciting news. As you know, the top three winners at our fair will go on to compete at the State Science Fair. The organizers made an announcement today that might make some of you extra interested in doing your best. Not only can you win a ribbon, but today they announced the winner at the state level will also win an all-expenses-paid trip to the NASA Camp Kennedy Space Center."

I could see Katie grip the edges of her desk. More

than anything in the world Katie wanted to be an astronaut. Well, first she planned to win a gold medal for gymnastics in the Olympics, but she figured she could do both. People started to whisper back and forth and I could tell Ms. Caul was happy to see us this excited about science. Normally we only got this worked up over recess.

"I'm totally going to win!" Nathan called out. "*Space Fighters* is my favorite movie of all time. I was born to be the captain of my own spaceship." He made *phew-phew* sounds while pretending to mow me down with his imaginary laser gun. A few of the other boys in class shot back at him. I rolled my eyes. Boys are weird.

"Hopefully, that gives all of you reasons to work extra hard on your projects before Friday," Ms. Caul said. "Now you can go to lunch."

"I didn't know they had camps in space," Paula said to her friend Miranda as they walked toward the door. "I wonder how they get the horses and cabins up there."

Katie dashed over to my desk. She was so excited she was bouncing on her tiptoes. "Oh my gosh, space camp! Did you know they have a launch simulator? And I heard you get to build robots too." She clutched my arm. "Not just any robots, real space robots."

"You're going to win, you have to. You're the best in science in our whole class." I wasn't even just saying this to be nice. Katie really was a science whiz. The model she made last year of the solar system with spray-painted foam balls was still hanging in one of the hallway display cases because it was that good. Her science project for this year had a space theme. She had started it months ago, as soon as she heard there would be a science fair. Even before Ms. Caul assigned it.

"I don't know, I bet a lot of people have done cool stuff," Katie said, looking nervous.

"You won't have to worry about mine." I had a hard time coming up with a good idea. I'd finally decided on a project with plants, but it wasn't working very well. I couldn't figure out what I was doing wrong, but I was 100 percent sure it wasn't going to be a winner. "My project is pretty lame," I admitted.

"Hey, Willow, if you wanted we could work together on a project," Nathan offered as he came up behind me. "Then we would win for sure."

I raised an eyebrow. Nathan wasn't someone who had a confidence problem. I couldn't figure him out. Sometimes he tried hard to annoy me by doing things like stealing my notebook or throwing French fries at my head. Other times Nathan would do nice things, like letting me use the good bat when playing softball in gym, or hanging my coat next to the heater in our cloak room so that it would be all warm and dry when it was time to go home. Humdrum boys are very confusing.

"Now that I know the prize is so cool, I'm going to come up with a killer project," Nathan said. "I'd let you be my partner if you wanted. Then when we win you can be the copilot of my spaceship."

"You know this is NASA right? It's not make-believe space, it's the real thing. There won't be any Jedi knights or star destroyers." I rolled my eyes at Katie, showing her what I thought of Nathan's big plan. I didn't want her to worry that I would try and beat her. I knew how important winning was for her.

"I'll be your partner," Bethany said to Nathan. Bethany was part of the popular group in our class, along with Paula and Miranda. Out of the three of them, Bethany was the snotty one. Miranda was popu-lar because she was pretty and nice. Paula was popu-lar because she hung out with Miranda. Bethany was popular because she was kind of scary.

Bethany had a crush on Nathan. I could tell because she was always sucking up to him and trying to be next to him in line when our class went anywhere. Bethany squished her way into the aisle so she was standing right next to Nathan, practically pushing me out of the way. "If you want to win, you should work with me. My dad is a surgeon and he's helping me with my project."

"You aren't supposed to have your parents do your project for you," I said, getting angry. "The whole point is that we're supposed to learn how to come up with a hypo . . . thissy . . ."

"Hypothesis," Katie corrected me, which just goes to show what a science whiz she is and why she deserves to win. She pays attention in class.

"Right, hypothesis. We're supposed to come up with our own one of those and then try and prove it. If your parents do all the work, then you aren't learning anything." I crossed my arms over my chest.

"Whatever," Bethany said, turning her back to me and faced Nathan. "Do you want to partner with me? I think you'd make a great star fleet captain. I've seen *Space Fighters* at least ten times. I always think how you remind me of the captain. You have to win that trip to space camp."

"I like the guy who is the space smuggler better than the captain," Nathan said.

I'd seen *Space Fighters* too and thought Nathan was a bit more like the smuggler in the movie, but I would never say it because I wasn't a kiss-up.

"Oh my gosh, you are just like that guy!" Bethany said, proving that she would rather kiss up than make any sense. I snorted.

Nathan's eyes narrowed and I could tell he was annoyed. He thought I was snorting about the idea of him being the smuggler. "Yeah, I'll be your partner," he said to Bethany. "That sounds like a great idea."

She squealed like they had already won the contest. She linked arms with Nathan and led him toward the cafeteria. "You'll have to come over to my house *every* day after school so we can work on this together with my dad."

"You guys better not cheat!" I called after them.

"You better prepare to be a loser!" Nathan yelled back.

I watched them walk arm in arm down the hall. "I can't believe Bethany. She doesn't care about science at all. She's only doing all this because she wants to suck up to Nathan." I shook my head in disbelief. "And did you see how quick Nathan agreed to be her partner? It was like he couldn't wait for her to ask."

"He did ask you first, but you sort of made fun of him," Katie pointed out.

"I wasn't making fun of *him*, I was explaining that being an astronaut and being a space smuggler are two completely different things. He shouldn't try and win if real space isn't important to him like it is to you. Besides, I bet Bethany can't even spell astronaut."

"Bethany probably can't spell her own name right. I think that's why she signs her name Beth on all her papers," Katie said, grabbing her lunch bag.

"We could totally use magic to make sure you win," I said, still angry with Nathan and Bethany. "I could make sure that your project is the best project that's ever been made. Not only will NASA invite you to camp, they'll invite you to be the youngest astronaut in their program. They'll let you run Mission Control. They'll name a shuttle after you."

Katie cut me off before I could come up with any more ideas. "First of all, NASA isn't making any more shuttles. Secondly, if I won by magic then it wouldn't be the same. I want to win because I have the best project, not because I cheated. Lastly, don't you remember? You're not supposed to use magic to help me. You promised the Fairy Council and your mom."

My mouth shut with a click. Katie was right on all three points. Sometimes it's hard to have a genius as a best friend. They're almost always right.

"So what do we do?" I asked. "We can't just let them win."

Katie smiled at me. "I don't plan to let them win. I plan to make the best science project ever and win fair and square."

We high-fived. I was proud she was my best friend. My stomach growled again.

"But first we should have lunch," I said.

"Good plan. Lunch first, then scientific glory." Katie linked arms with me and we headed off to the cafeteria.

four

If your science project isn't working the way you expected:

   a. You might have forgotten to do an important step.

   b. Your hypothesis could be wrong.

   c. You might just be lousy at science.

   d. A rogue garden gnome could be messing with you.

Answer:

The correct answer might not be what you're expecting!

My science project wasn't very exciting. I had four plants that my dad helped me set up in his greenhouse.

I was feeding the first plant water, another Miracle-Gro *and* water, the third plant tea, and the last plant Diet Coke. My theory was that the plant that was getting the water and plant food would do the best. The plant that was getting Diet Coke I expected to die. At the very least I expected the soda plant to be sort of unhealthy looking, limp with a few brown leaves. That's what I figured would happen. After all, it can't be good for anyone—humdrum, fairy, dog, or plant—to live on pop alone. However, that wasn't what was happening.

All four plants were fine. More than fine, they seemed to be growing. Their leaves were a nice dark green and almost looked like someone had polished each one. I went out to the greenhouse after school and inspected the plants again. They were definitely growing. Wait a minute! My finger stabbed at the pots. Someone had put in fresh dirt! Each plant was cradled by a pile of fresh, fluffy-looking soil. I looked around the greenhouse. There was a bag of dirt on the floor ripped open in the corner. It looked like someone had chewed through the bag. My dad would never have left his greenhouse looking like this. I crouched down to get a closer look. The dirt was everywhere. It was like someone dug through the bag and tossed the dirt over his shoulder. I could think of only one person I knew who was this messy. *And* he liked to dig.

"Winston!" I waited for him in the doorway with my arms crossed.

After a minute, Winston moseyed into the greenhouse. He plunked down and scratched his ear with his back paw while giving a giant yawn. "You're home from school already? Whoo . . . my afternoon nap must have run a bit long today. I really should start earlier."

"Is there anything you want to tell me?" I tapped my foot on the floor waiting for him to fess up. Maybe I would take a lesson from Katie's parents and see what he thought the punishment should be.

Winston scratched his ear again. "Nope. Is there something you want me to tell you?"

"Maybe you should think harder. There's something you need to tell me." I yanked my head over to the side toward the bag of potting soil. "I bet there's something on your mind."

Winston cocked his head to the side and seemed to think about it. "Well . . . the only thing really on my mind is that I could go for a snack."

"A snack?" I yelled. "That's all you can think of? What about the mess in here?"

Winston looked around the room as if he were noticing it for the first time. "It is sort of dirty. You should clean it up before your dad sees it."

"*I* should clean it up?" I huffed in annoyance. "Since you made the mess, don't you think *you* should be the one who does the cleaning?"

Winston backed up. "Me? I didn't make this mess. Don't get me wrong, I've made plenty of messes, but this one isn't mine."

"Then who dug through all the dirt? And messed with my plants?"

"Not me. If you want me to be honest, there is something I should confess, but it has nothing to do with your plants. You know that fancy pen you have with the flamingo on top and the feathers?" Winston wouldn't meet my eyes and instead looked down at his paws.

"The pen I haven't been able to find anywhere?" I asked.

"I might have chewed the feathers off and buried what remained of it under the bush by the front door."

"You might have." I raised an eyebrow.

"Okay, okay, I did it. I'm not a dog who is built for

a life of crime. I ate the pen. I blame the feathers. They were waving in the wind, taunting me."

I plopped down on the wooden bench. I believed him. Winston was a very honest dog. He was often naughty, but he would confess if you confronted him. If he had done something to my science project he would have said something. "Then who did this?"

Winston tried to jump up onto the bench, but smacked into the side and fell back to the floor. That's the problem with small dogs: They often forget they are small and try to do big-dog things. I leaned over and scooped him up and sat him down next to me.

"Could Lucinda be to blame? She was pretty mad about you ruining her first kiss by spying on her," Winston asked.

"Lucinda is capable of almost anything, but I don't think she would mess with school stuff. Plus this is dirt. Lucinda hates to get grimy." I picked up one of the potted plants and turned it in my hands. "Besides, it's like someone took the time to replant each one carefully. If Lucinda was trying to get even with me she would have just dumped them out of their planters or cut their leaves off. I thought maybe you dug them up and then were trying to cover up the crime."

EILEEN COOK

Winston huffed, the fur around his mouth puffing out. "Dogs always get blamed for everything."

I noticed something bright partly buried under a pile of dirt in the corner. I leaned over and pulled it out. It was a small red knit stocking cap. "Where did this come from? It looks like it's for a baby."

Winston's nose twitched. "It smells funny. I can't place it."

I slid the cap onto Winston's head and giggled. "It suits you." The cap covered his ears and pushed his bushy eyebrows down.

Winston shook his head until the cap flew off and back onto the floor. "I am not the kind of dog who likes to wear outfits." He sneezed. "And I'm telling you there's something funny about that . . ." Winston stopped midsentence with his ears pricked up. "Did you hear that?"

There was a skittering, rustling sound under the bench. I yanked my feet up. I didn't mind mice, but I wasn't crazy about the idea of a rat. There was another rustle and then something reached out and snatched the hat off the floor and pulled it under the bench. It happened so fast I couldn't tell what it was, but it didn't look like a rat.

"Did you see that?" I hissed to Winston. "Do something."

Winston had backed up into the corner of the bench against the wall. "Me? Why me? You're bigger."

"You're supposed to be a guard dog."

Winston's tail was tucked under his behind. He gave a wimpy-sounding bark. "Okay, I did my part, now you check to see if it's gone."

If I ever got another dog I was going to get something like a German Shepherd. I stood up on the bench and grabbed the rake. I took a couple deep breaths and then jumped off the bench as far as I could. I whirled around and held the rake in front of me like a sword. Nothing moved. I couldn't see under the bench because it was too dark. I poked under the bench with the rake. Something strong grabbed the tines of the rake and pulled it out of my hands.

Winston squealed like a little girl and covered his eyes with his paws. I grabbed for the handle of the rake and pulled it back. "Who's under there?" I said, trying to sound brave. My brain scrambled to try and think of some sort of spell I could use, but I was afraid I would either cover whatever-it-was with glitter or make it larger. I really needed to start paying more attention in my spell workshops on the weekends.

"If you want me to come out then stop poking me," a gruff voice said from under the bench.

I dropped the rake in surprise. I hadn't expected it to speak. There was another rustling sound and then out from under the bench crawled a tiny person, no more than a foot tall, with a long white beard. He was dressed in blue wool pants and a baggy linen shirt. He jammed his red knit cap onto his head.

Winston's mouth fell open in shock. The little man whacked him on the nose. "What are you staring at, you furry beast? Your mouth gaping open like that means you'll catch flies."

Uh-oh. We had a garden gnome.

five

True or False:

Garden gnomes are nothing more than cute statues that old people like to put in their yards.

Answer:

False. Gnomes are mythical creatures who love the outdoors. They often hide in humdrum gardens and parks, and enjoy taking care of the plants. However, while they look sort of cute and roly-poly, they can be darn cranky. Also, if you want something for your garden I think pink flamingos look nicer.

Winston growled at the gnome. Now that he could see it was something his size he'd decided he wasn't afraid.

"Don't you growl at me, you hairy monster, you

digger of holes!" the gnome yelled at Winston. He brushed the dirt off his pants.

"What is it?" Winston said leaning over the bench to sniff the cap.

"It's a gnome. I've seen pictures in books and my Uncle Sebastian has one named Larry that lives in his yard."

"'It?' I am not an 'it.'" The gnome shook his dirt encrusted finger at me. "My name is Jakob DeGroot."

"Nice to meet you, Jakob," I said hoping he'd forgotten about me poking him with the rake. It's a well-known fact you don't want to get on a gnome's bad side. Gnomes like to play tricks on humdrums and fairies.

"I would say it was nice to meet you, but it has been anything but pleasant." He brushed his hands off and pushed past me. He crawled up the shelves so he could stand on the counter. He looked at my science fair plants and sighed. He refluffed the dirt where my fingers had pressed it back down.

"Are you the one who's been messing with my science project?" I asked.

"Me? Messing with them?" Jakob shook his head as if he couldn't believe what I was saying. "I haven't messed with these plants—I've saved their very lives."

"But the whole point of my science project is to see what happens if I feed the plants different things," I explained.

Jakob grabbed the plant and held it to his chest like it was a baby. "What happens? You know what happens? You kill them. That's what happens." He looked at me as if he were disgusted. "Plant killer."

"I'm not a plant killer," I said. Jakob looked at me with one giant, white, bushy eyebrow raised.

"Okay, it might seem like I'm a plant killer, but what I'm doing is for science."

"Do you think that makes it okay? Would it be okay if I poked you in the eye with a stick, as long as the reason that I did it was because I wanted to know—for science of course—what would happen?" Jakob paced up and down on the counter, kicking tiny clots of dirt out of his way. "Or maybe I'll shave your dog to see what he would look like naked. That sounds like a good science experiment. Who wants to see what the dog looks like under all that fur?"

Winston growled. "Now wait a minute. Let's not get crazy. It isn't even funny to joke about shaving a dog."

"No one's shaving anybody," I said, trying to calm Winston down before he bit Jakob. I had enough issues with the Fairy Council without having a magical creature filing a complaint about me for having a violent dog.

"Oh, ho . . . so that's how it is. It's fine if *you* want to do science by killing plants, but if I want to do science by shaving one little dog, it's forbidden. Each night I've had to wash and rinse the roots of this plant to remove the fizzy drink you keep applying. It takes me hours. And do you appreciate what I've done? No."

"The plants look great, but they aren't your plants. There must be other plants that need your help. There's a tree near my school that looks like it could use some gnome assistance. A few of the leaves are brown."

Jakob drew himself up so he was standing tall. Well, as tall someone who was shorter than a large cat could stand. "I am not your personal gardener. If you think the tree needs some help then I suggest you do something about it yourself." He shook his head like he couldn't believe how dumb I was. "It's quite clear that gardening is not your special skill. If you don't know these basics then I'm not sure what it is you're covering in this science class of yours."

I sighed. "Fine. Forget the tree at my school, but you also have to leave my plants alone. I'm going to lock the greenhouse from now on." I took my plant out of his hands.

Jakob grabbed the plant back.

I snatched it again.

Jakob's eyes narrowed and he tried to yank it back, only I wouldn't let go this time. I held the plant above my head where he didn't stand a chance of reaching it.

Jakob put his hands on his hips. "Oh, that's mature. You think it's funny to make fun of someone because they're short? Is that what they're teaching you sprites in school these days? I can tell you, when I was a young gnome we had respect for our elders."

"I bet when you were a young gnome, people used horses and buggies instead of cars," Winston grumbled.

"Very funny. I suppose someone with no thumbs has to rely on humor to get by," Jakob fired back.

"I think you should go," I said. Winston gave another growl. Jakob stared at me as if he were trying to memorize my face.

"Fine. I'll be on my way." He plopped down on the counter and started to lower himself down to the ground.

"Do you want some help?" I offered. He really was a tiny little guy. I didn't want to fight with him. I only wanted him to leave my things alone.

Jakob dropped the rest of the way to the floor and brushed off his pants. "I don't need any help. You're the one who's going to need help. If you think I'll be forgetting about this, then you are wrong. Jakob DeGroot doesn't forget an insult!" The gnome used both hands to push the door open and slipped out of the greenhouse without another word.

Winston jumped down off the bench and sniffed all around the floor like he wanted to make sure he was really gone. "What do we do now?" he asked.

I took a deep breath. "I'm going to have to start my project over and hope no one notices. It doesn't really matter too much, it's not like I want to win. I'm hoping Katie wins, but I still need to do a good job so I don't let Ms. Caul down. I figure if I have to, I could give the one plant triple doses of Diet Coke."

"I didn't mean what to do with the science project. I meant what do we do about Jakob? He sounded to me like he meant business."

"I'll keep the greenhouse locked from now on. And I'll talk to my dad. I think he's had more experience with gnomes. He might know what to do." I shrugged. "Besides, how much trouble could he make? He's pretty small."

Winston gave a disgusted sniff. "You should never underestimate someone because of their size. Small people can cause big trouble."

Winston sometimes might be silly enough to chase his own tail, but in this instance he was smarter than Einstein.

six

A good science project would be:

   a. a working replica of a Mars rover made from a Barbie car and Legos.

   b. a giant scale model of a human heart (that clearly someone's dad made for them, which counts as cheating).

   c. one where you spelled all the words correctly on your poster.

   d. anything that hasn't been screwed up by a cranky garden gnome.

The science fair was held in the school gym. Our gym teacher Mr. Mathis wandered around the room with his whistle. He kept mumbling about how all the tables better not scratch the floor. I suspected he didn't like all this science. He thought sports were the most important thing in the world. I was glad to get a few days off from gym. We were playing dodgeball, and Bethany always tried to hit me with the red rubber ball hard enough to leave a mark.

After lunch we set up our science projects and had a chance to see what everyone else had made. The judging wouldn't be until tomorrow morning, so everyone's parents could come.

I'd done the best I could with my plants for the past couple of days, but the one plant still looked far healthier than it should have. Katie set up her project next to mine. She'd made a copy of a Mars rover out of her old pink Barbie car and some LEGOs. It looked good enough for NASA.

"Check it out," she said using the remote control to drive the rover back and forth across the gym floor. "I bought a LEGO robot kit online, but I put it together all by myself."

"Wow." I knew Katie would come up with something cool, but she'd made her very own robot. I hadn't even been able to kill a plant.

"I love that your robot's pink," Paula said. She was setting up her project on the table on my other side. "I think space would be way cooler if there was better stuff. Everything is white, black, or gray. And those space suits the astronauts wear are super bulky. I think they make everyone look kinda fat."

"They need to be bulky because they have all sorts of life-support systems in them. There's no air in space," Katie explained. "They don't really build them for looks."

"You would think with all those scientists they could come up with a way to make them look good while they keep you alive. You know, I'm really interested in astronomy and stuff too. It's what I did my project on." Paula straightened her poster for her display.

Katie and I stood in front of her poster. It showed all the horoscope signs and what they meant.

"What's your sign?" Paula asked Katie.

"Leo."

"That makes you a leader. Also," Paula explained while looking down at her notes, "it means the sun is your ruling star."

"Um, Paula?" Katie said. "Did you know astronomy and astrology are two different things? Astronomy is the study of the stars. Astrology isn't really science."

"It isn't?" Paula's shoulders slumped and her lower lip started to tremble. "I was so sure. Why do they make them sound so much alike if they don't want people to confuse them?"

"It is stupid they made those words so similar. Anyone could screw them up. Besides, it's still an awesome poster," Katie said, then nudged me with her elbow.

"Oh yeah, it's totally awesome. I like how you drew all the signs. The Pisces one is especially nice with all the fish scales," I offered. I didn't mention that Taurus the bull looked a bit like a moose.

Bethany shoved me to the side so she could throw her arm around Paula. "Have you seen our project? Nathan and I are going to win for sure. I'm already planning what I'll bring with me to space camp." Bethany pointed across the aisle. Nathan was standing next to their table with his hands shoved in his pockets and a scowl on his face.

"Holy moly," Paula said.

Paula wasn't always right about things, for example she thought sharks and dolphins were the same animal only sharks were the mean ones, but this time she was right. It was impressive. Bethany and Nathan's project was a giant clear plastic heart. It had red and blue labels for the various parts.

"Go ahead, Nathan, plug it in," Bethany said. Nathan didn't do anything except keep scowling, so Bethany bent down under the table and plugged the heart in. For a second nothing happened, but then the inside started beating, and red water started to move through the different parts of the plastic heart. "I can speed it up to show what it looks like if the person is running."

Katie looked at the plastic heart and then back at her Barbie rover. I could tell she was discouraged. The heart even made a sort of thumping sound. It looked like something you might make if you had been in college for a thousand years.

"You didn't make that on your own," I said. There was no way anyone could believe Bethany made this on her own. She never paid attention in science, and in art class when she drew a horse it always looked like a walrus. If she had made the heart it would have looked more like a blob. Bethany's dad was a doctor. He probably made the heart in medical school. "The rules say you have to do the project on your own."

"How do you know I didn't make it? Besides, it looks like all you did was dig stuff out of your yard."

"At least I dug them up myself." I made myself stand up straight. My project might not be that good, but at least I hadn't cheated.

"Oooh, really impressive science, digging stuff up," Bethany rolled her eyes at Nathan. "It's a good thing you worked with me, Nathan, otherwise you would have had to go gardening with the loser."

My eyes narrowed and I said a quick spell under my breath.

"Give it a rest, Bethany," Nathan said.

Bethany opened her mouth to say something else, but she suddenly hiccupped. She covered her mouth with her hand and I smiled. She was about to discover that these particular hiccups were going to be difficult to get rid of.

"Hey, did you know astronomy and astrology are two different things?" Paula asked Nathan.

Bethany stuck her finger in my face before Nathan could talk. "You're—*hic*—just jealous—*hic*—because you—*hic*—know we're going—*hic*—to win. *Hic, hic, hic, hic.*"

"You should get some water for those hiccups. I've heard there are some people who have those for years," I said.

"Come on, I want to see what the fifth graders made." Katie pulled me away from Bethany and down another aisle.

"Can you believe she cheated?" I shook my head. "No wonder she had to partner with someone else. There's no way she could explain that on her own."

"Did you give her the hiccups?" Katie asked.

I giggled. "Yep." I looked over to see if Katie was mad. "The spell will wear off in a few hours." I liked the idea of Bethany spending the rest of her day hiccupping and maybe even having her mom take her to the doctor to check it out. I hoped Katie wouldn't want me to cancel the spell too quickly.

"You should've made it so she couldn't stop farting," Katie said. "Can you imagine her trying to cover that up with Nathan around?" We started laughing. Katie almost always had the best ideas. Bethany should be glad that I was the one with the magic instead of Katie. A supergenius with magic could be a very dangerous enemy. I wondered if this is what the Fairy Council was afraid of: the kind of trouble the two of us could get in together.

"All right, everyone!" Principal Doyle called out. She was the coolest principal in the whole world. She never yelled, even if you had done something you really shouldn't, and she cared about every student at Riverside. She was also my grandma, so that made her extra special as far as I was concerned. "We'll see everyone back here tomorrow morning for the judging." Grandma smiled at everyone. "It looks like the judges will have a hard time; there are some really nice projects."

Everyone headed for the doors. Katie and I linked arms. I was invited to her house for dinner. Her mom was making pizza, which was my favorite (no pepperoni, but extra cheese and mushrooms).

"See you—*hic*—tomorrow, losers—*HIC*," Bethany said, once we were all outside.

I opened my mouth to say something back, like how I might lose the science fair but at least I could finish a sentence without hiccupping, but then someone touched my arm. It was Nathan.

"Don't let her get to you. I thought your project was pretty cool," he said.

I stared at him. My project? I could see thinking Katie's project was cool, but mine? Was he blind? All I had were four plants. "I guess you're pretty happy with how your heart turned out," I said.

"Listen . . . about my project," Nathan started to say, but then Katie grabbed my arm so hard I almost fell over.

"Willow has to go," Katie said dragging me down the sidewalk.

"I just wanted to tell her . . ." Nathan was standing in the middle of the sidewalk, confused.

"Sorry, no time. You can talk to her tomorrow." Katie pulled me farther away.

"Wait a minute, I wanted to hear what he was going to say," I tried to pull back, but Katie can be very strong when she wants to be. It's all the handsprings she does in her gymnastics class.

"Trust me, you have to see this," Katie pulled me around the corner and pointed to the building.

I looked at the school. At first I couldn't figure out what Katie wanted me to look at, but then I saw a flash of red in the corner of one of the windows. Oh, no. I knew that hat.

Jakob the gnome was inside the school. He pressed his tiny little hands against the glass and stuck his tongue out at me.

I broke free from Katie's grasp and ran up to the window. I pounded on the glass. "What are you doing in there?"

"That's the gnome you were telling me about, isn't it?" Katie asked. "I mean even if you hadn't described him I probably would have guessed. He looks just like one of those garden statues except for all the rude gestures." Jakob pressed his butt on the window and shook it in our faces. "Besides, before I knew you were a fairy I never saw anything like this."

"He's going to mess with my science fair project," I said to Katie. "I should have known he would try something. Can you keep watch while I go back in to find him?" I pounded on the glass again. "Come out of there!"

"Is everything okay?"

Katie and I whirled around to see Nathan standing there. My arms dropped to my side. "I can explain him," I said. I wasn't sure how I was going to explain it, but Katie was right next to me and she wanted to be a writer when she grew up so I was counting on her coming up with something.

"Explain who?" Nathan asked. "The statue?"

I spun back around. Jakob had frozen in place with his hands on his hips and a big fake smile spread across his face. He looked like every other fake gnome statue you saw in people's gardens. "Um, yeah. I brought the statue to go with my plants for my project."

"Like a good luck charm," Katie added.

"Right. Like a good luck charm, only I just remembered that I left him there and now I realize that I shouldn't leave him in the school overnight."

"Why?"

"Because someone might steal him," I explained. I didn't add that anyone who stole this particular garden gnome was in for a very unpleasant surprise.

"People steal gnomes all the time," Katie said. "You hear about this stuff on the Internet. They pose them in strange places and take pictures. It's cruel."

"You don't have to worry. No one is going to steal him. The janitor is locking up the school now," Nathan said.

I looked at Katie and then took off running for the front door of the school. I tore around the corner and saw Mr. Hooper, the janitor, locking the front door. I pounded up the stairs. I was breathing so hard at first I couldn't talk. I had to bend over to try and catch my breath. "I forgot something," I gasped.

"You'll have to get it tomorrow. We're all locked up for now," Mr. Hooper said, shaking his giant ring of keys as proof.

"It will only take me a minute," I promised.

"Sorry, can't have kids locked in school after hours." He started to close the door and I shoved my sneaker in the gap.

"Wait! Can you get my grandma for me? It's really important that I talk with her."

"Principal Doyle left a few minutes ago. She had a meeting right after school." Mr. Hooper patted my head, ruffling my hair. "In my day, kids could hardly wait to get out of school, they weren't fighting to get back in, like you." He chuckled. "You run along home now."

"Wait!" I called out, but Mr. Hooper didn't wait, he just shut the door in my face, the latch making a loud clicking sound as it locked.

Jakob was inside. I had no idea what he would get up to, but I was 100 percent sure it wouldn't be good.

seven

If a cranky gnome who has it out for you is left alone all night in your school he might:

a. burn it down.

b. spray paint your name on the lockers with a goofy-looking picture of you next to it.

c. replant your science project so that it was growing out of the basketball hoop, which will make Mr. Mathis, the gym teacher, supermad, and he'll make you do extra laps.

d. something even worse than you can imagine, even if you are really, really, really good at imagining bad things.

Answer:

D. I repeat: Something even worse than you can

imagine, even if you are an Olympic champion imaginer.

Saturday morning I was at school a full hour before it was supposed to open for the science fair. I pressed my face up against the glass doors and peered in. Nothing in the hallway looked different. I hadn't slept very well last night. I had lain in bed staring up at the ceiling thinking of all the different kinds of trouble Jakob might cause. Gnomes didn't have a lot of hobbies. They're too small to go bowling or play soccer. If you kicked a ball to a gnome it would knock him right over. They could be crushed by a bowling ball, and they're too short to go to the movies. They can't see over the seat in front of them. The only thing gnomes do for fun is take care of plants and cause trouble.

Finally, I saw Mr. Hooper coming down the hallway. He would stop every few feet to pick something off the floor or to wipe a mark off one of the lockers. I was practically bouncing off the door waiting for him. If he were any slower he would be moving backward. He pulled his giant key ring off his belt and started to fumble through the keys looking for the one that would open the door. The judges would be arriving any minute. I had to get in there and make sure everything was okay.

Mr. Hooper clicked the door open and chuckled when he saw me. "Well, aren't you the early bird today? You hoping to catch a worm?"

I dashed past him and ran down the hall to the gym. "I'm hoping to catch something!"

I slid into the gym, my feet squeaking on the floor. I looked around the room, but nothing looked out of place. "Jakob?" I hissed. I ran over to the bank of windows where I had seen him with Katie, but he wasn't there. I bent down and looked under the first row of tables, but there was no sign of him. Not seeing him was almost worse than seeing him.

"Where are you?" I said.

The sound of laughter came from the hallway. It was Ms. Caul with the judges. There wasn't any more time to look for Jakob. I dashed down the aisle to where my project was set up to see what he might have done. I was three or four tables away when I saw it.

Oh my gosh.

My plant project had gone completely wild. There was dirt mounded onto the table and spilling onto the floor. All four of the plants had grown overnight. Like,

Jack-and-the-Beanstalk growth. One of them was as thick as a telephone pole and it was snaking down the aisle, winding up and around the table legs. It knocked over a trash can at the end of the row. Another plant had leaves the size of Volkswagens. One leaf made a green tent above Paula's horoscope poster. She could have camped under it and stayed dry during a thunderstorm.

Then I saw what my plants had done to Katie's project. I swallowed and then walked up closer so I could see every horrible detail. The plant's tendrils had wound itself all over her robot like a spider web. The only way I could even tell her robot was under there was one tire in the front that still wasn't covered, and there were places where the pink Barbie car peeked through the green. There was no way the robot would be able to run. It was so covered it wouldn't move an inch. The judges wouldn't be able to see any of the hard work she had put in. There would be no way she could win. She might even be disqualified. It was okay my project was ruined: I was the one who made Jakob mad, but Katie was innocent.

I grabbed at the plant, pulling it off Katie's project. I had to try and fix it. I pulled three or four handfuls of leaves off the robot. It hardly made a dent.

I heard voices in the hallway. People were starting to arrive! I snatched as many vines off as possible.

"We can start the judging over here," Ms. Caul said.

There was no more time. The judges were going to come around the corner any minute. I knew I wasn't supposed to do any magic, but if there was ever an emergency, this was it. I said a quick spell. There was a *POP* sound and then the plants shrank. They were still way too large, but at least Katie's rover was uncovered. I took a deep breath. Whew. Everything was going to be okay.

"Willow Thalia Doyle!"

I spun around. My grandma was standing there with the tallest, skinniest woman you have ever seen. Her mouth was open in a perfect circle. It was one of the members of the Fairy Council, Miss Pipkins. And there was no mistaking it: Both of them had seen me do the spell. Even though I knew I was caught, I couldn't stop the words that flew out of my mouth.

"I didn't do anything."

Grandma turned her head to the side and looked at me.

"I mean, I just did a small spell and I had to," I explained.

"I thought we were clear there was to be no magic allowed," Miss Pipkins said. She puckered her mouth together like she was sucking on a lemon. "None."

"There's this gnome," I started to say.

Grandma put her hand on my shoulder and squeezed. "This isn't the time or place to have this discussion."

"I know we were perfectly clear on this magic issue," Miss Pipkins said. "We had at least two meetings about it, and then another meeting to make sure we were all in agreement. There was to be absolutely no magic between this sprite and the humdrum." She shook her head back and forth. She looked like an angry praying mantis with her long arms and legs, and her green suit.

"I'm sure we can sort this all out in my office." Grandma looked around and smiled at the group of judges coming down the aisle. "We don't need to discuss magic and spells with so many humdrums around," she said as she led us out of the gym.

"I should call the rest of the council. We're going to need an emergency meeting to discuss this." Miss Pipkins clucked like she was upset, but I could tell she was excited too. She seemed like the kind of person who was a big fan of meetings and agendas. I bet she was a list maker, too. She looked like someone who would like crossing things off with a big *swoosh* of her pen.

I shuffled down the hall to Grandma's office. I could tell this was one of those times when no matter how much I explained, it wasn't going to be good enough. This is why no one has a gnome as a best friend.

eight

True or False:

If you are told by the Fairy Council that you shouldn't do any magic for your humdrum best friend, but then you have a really, really, really good reason to do magic, they will understand.

Answer:

False. Fairy councils, much like many grown-ups, have TOTALLY forgotten what it was like to be ten.

I sat in Grandma's office, staring down at her rug. It was a flying carpet, although she never took it out because she said it was too unreliable. Foreign import. If there was any way for me to get the carpet out from under her heavy wooden desk, I would have taken my chances with the rug and flown right out of there. I would have risked the faulty brake system. I wasn't interested in stopping anyway.

"Gnomes," Grandma said after I finished explaining. Her nose wrinkled up. "I know we should like all magical creatures, but their tiny little hands and how they sort of scurry around gives me the shivers. My friend, Josephine, had so many in her garden that she had to get an exterminator to capture them and release them in a park across town."

"And they're mean!" I pointed out. "They weren't Jakob's plants to start with, and when I explained to him how I needed to use them for my science experiment he didn't care." I was officially adding gnomes to my list of magical creatures I didn't like very much. I also wasn't very fond of unicorns. One summer my parents had sent me to sprite camp. I'd been really excited about learning how to ride a unicorn, but it wasn't as much fun as I thought. They were really big, and it was hard to stay on. The unicorns could tell if you weren't confident, and they would buck and toss you up and off. I spent more time hitting the ground after being thrown than I did riding them. Then they would come over and poke you with their horns and laugh. Unicorns can be snotty.

Miss Pipkins twisted the giant blue ring on her finger. Even her hands were skinny, like a bundle of twigs. "I have no idea what the rest of the council is going to say when they hear about this. Magic used willy-nilly."

"Now, the council can't hold Willow responsible for what this gnome's done." Grandma tidied the folders lined up on her desk. "Granted, her science project has gone a bit haywire, but I don't think there's any damage that can't be fixed."

"A bit?" Miss Pipkins sniffed. "One of those plants could have filled a jungle all by itself."

"It's a science fair, we'll find a way to explain it," Grandma said. I nodded. I was sure she would be able to come up with something. She didn't get to be a Fairy Godmother Level 3 without coming up with more than one way to cover up magic that had gone wrong. My grandma could do anything.

"Can I go now?" I asked, standing up. I wanted to see what the judges thought of Katie's project. I still had my fingers crossed that she'd win a place at the state science fair so she'd have a chance at the big prize.

Miss Pipkins poked me with her skinny finger until I sat back down. "Don't you think there is some further explaining to do? This isn't simply about the gnome, it's also about what you did. Was it, or was it not, made very clear that you were not allowed to do magic that would impact this humdrum friend of yours,"—Miss Pipkins looked at her clipboard—"Katherine Hillegonds?"

"Katie. No one calls her Katherine."

Miss Pipkins ignored me. "My records show that we discussed this forbidding of magic at no fewer than three meetings, *and* a written document of this ruling was provided to you. Both you and your parents signed it as well. There were three copies of this document, and we even used the official fancy seal."

"I know, but—," I started to say.

"Do you need to see a copy of that document to refresh your memory?" Miss Pipkins looked down her nose at me.

"I'm sure Willow knows what she did was wrong," Grandma said.

"Isn't it enough that we have to sort out what to do with a humdrum who knows we exist, without a barely trained sprite going off granting her wishes here and there?" Miss Pipkins sighed like she was very tired.

Maybe if she went to fewer meetings and ate more donuts, she'd be happier.

"I wasn't just granting silly wishes, like making sure she had never-ending candy bars, or that her bed would be made every morning by magic. I didn't even grant a wish! This was an emergency!" I explained.

Miss Pipkins rolled her eyes. "A science fair emergency, of course."

I bit my lip to avoid telling Miss Pipkins that it wasn't nice to make fun of things that are important to other people. I tried again to explain. "Katie worked really hard on her project. She wants to be an astronaut when she grows up, so going to space camp is a big deal to her. Her project was totaled, she didn't stand a chance."

"This humdrum is in fourth grade. She's too young to know what she really wants. It's just as likely that she would want to be a princess when she grows up."

"I'm not sure that's fair, Miss Pipkins," Grandma said. "Katie is a very special humdrum. While I agree that Willow shouldn't have broken the rule about using magic until the committee had a chance to explore the situation, she did it for the right reasons."

"There's never a good reason to break a rule." Miss Pipkins pulled her clipboard out of her bag and began making notes. "It's clear this surprise inspection was a good idea. I won't finish my report until tomorrow, but you can be assured it will not be positive." She underlined something she had written with a loud *swoosh* of her pen.

"Now, Miss Pipkins, there's no need to be hasty." Grandma pulled a box out of her desk. "Why don't we have a nice cup of tea and a cookie and discuss the situation. Surely you remember being a sprite. You know how difficult it can be at that age."

Miss Pipkins paused. The end of her thin, knobby nose twitched. They were toffee and chocolate chip cookies from my mom's bakery, Enchanted Sugar. My mom's baking was pretty much irresistible to fairies or humdrums. "Well, I couldn't lie about what I've seen today."

"Of course not." Grandma pushed the box of cookies a bit closer to her. "You need to tell them what you've seen, but we both know how you phrase things will make quite a difference. With all your experience you have a lot of influence on the council."

Miss Pipkins leaned over and picked up a cookie with her skinny chopstick fingers. "I suppose there's no reason to be too harsh. I remember my sprite years had their ups and downs as well. I was teased a fair bit."

I wasn't surprised that Miss Pipkins had been teased when she was in the fairy academy. Anyone who looked like a praying mantis and had a name like Gertrude Pipkins was bound to be called a few names.

Miss Pipkins nibbled on her cookie. "As long as Willow is willing to admit she was wrong, and that she knows now she shouldn't have done it, I'm sure I can find a way to write this inspection report in a way that won't be *too* harmful." She smiled and waited.

I fidgeted in my seat. "I know what I did was against the rules," I said.

"And?" Miss Pipkins raised her eyebrows. She must have plucked them all away, because her eyebrows were drawn on her face, two thin brown lines.

I chewed on my lower lip. "I can't say that I wouldn't do it again, that would be a lie. Katie's my best friend. I had to save her project."

Miss Pipkins's cookie crumbled in her hand. "I beg your pardon? Are you refusing to apologize?"

"I can't be sorry for doing what I think was right. It wasn't Katie's fault the gnome was mad at me. It wasn't fair her project was ruined. Space camp is her dream."

Miss Pipkins stood up so quickly her clipboard clattered to the floor. "Well, I never . . ." She huffed and puffed as if she couldn't think of words to describe how bad she thought I was. "It's clear to me that you think, as a sprite—a sprite who hasn't even passed Level 4, mind you—that you know better than the entire Fairy Council about what should be done."

"I'm not saying that, but I know my best friend better than anyone on the council. I know it was against the rules, but rules can be wrong sometimes," I insisted.

"I've heard enough." Miss Pipkins gathered up her jacket.

Grandma stood, "Let's not get upset. Let me get the tea going and have another cookie."

"Ms. Doyle, it's obvious you're taking your grand-daughter's side on this issue. It leaves me wondering if you are able to handle this situation. It's possible you're too close to those involved."

Grandma stood straighter. "I can assure you, Miss Pipkins, I have been working with humdrum children and sprites for my entire career. I feel very capable of overseeing this situation."

Miss Pipkin rummaged through her straw handbag. "I'm afraid I'm going to have to use my authority here." She pulled out a metal badge and held it up. It looked like one of those fake FBI badges you can buy in a toy store if you wanted to play cops and robbers. She waved it in front of our faces.

"Let's not blow this situation out of proportion," Grandma said.

There was a loud *BAM* and a bright flash of red and purple. I blinked my eyes over and over. There was something wrong. My mouth felt dry and it tasted like copper shavings. I looked myself over, but I didn't see anything different. I felt funny: My fingers felt numb, like my hands were falling asleep. I wondered if Miss Pipkin had done something like turn my hair pink.

Grandma fell back in her chair. She looked pale. I rushed over to her. "Are you okay?" I asked. I picked up a folder off her desk and fanned her.

"Goodness," Grandma said. "I'll be all right. I just feel a bit dizzy."

I whirled around to face Miss Pipkins. "What did you do?"

"I haven't done anything that I shouldn't. The Fairy Council allows me to do this. You can look it up under Section 14.5.2, subsection C, enforcement in extreme circumstances." Miss Pipkins tied her jacket belt tighter. "If you wish to appeal this decision, you'll have to take it up with the council."

"Let me guess, they'd have to schedule a meeting," Grandma said softly.

"Well, of course they would need a meeting. The council doesn't do things higgledy-piggledy."

I was still confused. I didn't understand what had happened. "What's Section 14.5.2?"

"I see someone not only uses magic when she shouldn't, but she also hasn't memorized the fairy hand-book." Miss Pipkins shook her finger at me. "I have no hope for your generation. Why, when I was a sprite, I could have quoted every chapter of that handbook."

Grandma touched my hand. "Section 14.5.2 is a punishment. It means she's taken away our magic. Neither of us can do a single spell until the council decides to give us our powers back."

I gasped. No magic? It didn't seem possible. Quickly, I tried to fly. Nothing. I didn't move. I didn't even float a few inches. I said a quick spell to make the cookies on the desk shoot up into the air, but they stayed right on the desk. Grandma smiled sadly at me and patted my hand.

There was a knock on the door and Miss Pipkins jumped. Ms. Caul leaned in the door and smiled at all of us. "There you are, Willow! You should come down to the gym to collect your ribbon."

"Ribbon?" I was confused.

"You're science project came in third. You're going to the state competition." She laughed when she saw my face. "No need to look upset. This is good news. You'll be happy to know that Katie came in second so you two can go together."

"Who came in first?" I asked.

"Bethany and Nathan, for their heart project."

Figures. Just when I thought my day couldn't get any worse.

nine

If you plan to keep something very personal (like the fact that your magic has been unfairly taken from you by a Fairy Council member who doesn't listen to reason) a secret, then you can count on:

    a. it staying a secret.

    b. people finding out something happened, but not the details.

    c. everything coming out.

Answer:

C. You might as well have taken a full-page ad in the newspaper and hour-long commercials on every TV station. Even penguins on the South Pole will know what happened. If there were people on the moon, they would know about it too.

I couldn't believe my parents were making me go to my Saturday sprite spell class. My parents kept pointing out how I promised to go to these classes in return for them letting me go to humdrum school and that just because I lost my magic didn't mean I could change the deal. Either my parents have totally forgotten what it was like to be a kid, or they had it hard as kids and they think these kinds of situations will make me a better grown-up one day. I've never understood why being miserable now was supposed to teach me how to be a better grown-up later. When I'm a parent I'm never going to be mean to my kids like this. I also won't make them eat Brussels sprouts. I'm taking notes so I never forget what it's like to be a kid.

I dragged my feet as I walked along the sidewalk. Maybe there would be a giant storm and a tornado would sweep me away before I could get there. Or I could be kidnapped by a wandering circus and forced to clean up after their elephants for the rest of my life. That would teach my parents. They would appreciate me once I was gone. Every time they saw an elephant they would cry about how they missed me, and how they would treat me so much better if they had a chance to do it all over again.

I could only imagine what the other sprites would say if they found out I'd lost my magic. I didn't know any sprites who had had the council take away their abilities. Usually they only took away powers from fairy godmothers who had really messed up. All I had done was save Katie's science project and everyone was acting like I borrowed a dragon and used him to burn down a humdrum town. I kicked a rock and watched it fly down the sidewalk. Winston, who was walking with me, whimpered.

"Sorry, I don't know what you're saying. Until the council changes their minds I can't understand a word." I kicked another rock. "It's like everyone wants to torture me."

Winston harrumphed. Even though I couldn't understand him I was willing to bet he was accusing me of being too dramatic. This coming from a dog who acted like it was a national emergency when we ran out of dog biscuits. You would think his fur was on fire the way he behaved when the box was empty.

I stopped outside the gate to the fairy academy. No tornados or circus kidnapping. I was going to have to go in. I had the worst luck. "Wait for me here?" I asked Winston. He wagged his tail. I guess that meant he would wait. Or that he was happy I was going inside. It could also mean he had seen a squirrel across the street and was already planning to chase it. Trying to figure out what was running through Winston's mind without being able to talk to him was a mystery. I looked at my watch. I'd walked as slowly as possible but there was still time before our spell workshop started. "Do you think the other sprites will be able to tell what happened when they look at me?"

Winston nudged my leg with his nose and made a sympathetic sound.

"My mom said no one would know I've lost my magic unless I tell them. She might have said that just to make me feel better." I looked at Winston. "Moms do that kind of thing, you know, tell you lies to make you do something they want. It's like when she told me I would like cauliflower if I tried it at least five times. I tried it six, just to be sure, and I still think it tastes like dirty socks. Turns out, she made up the part about me liking it."

Winston thumped his tail on the sidewalk in sympathy. He didn't like cauliflower either. Once I had tried to feed him some under the dinner table and he had spit it out on the kitchen floor. I rubbed his ears and slipped inside the building.

I cracked open the door to our classroom, and Sasha nearly mowed me down. She was floating at full speed.

"Oops, sorry." Adele flew to the end of the classroom and held up her hands to catch a humming blue energy ball that bounced off her hands and fired back toward Sasha who was standing on her chair.

"Hey, Willow, you can be on our team. It's girls against guys!" Sasha hit the ball so that it hovered up near the ceiling.

Milo said a quick spell and a shot of red light came out of his hands and deflected the ball. "Ha! It's ours now!" Milo attempted to pass the energy ball to Jordan. Adele flew in front of the ball and fired it over to me.

I had no magic to deflect the ball. It hit me square in the center of the chest. The energy in the ball threw me back, knocking me over a desk and onto the floor with a crash. I hit my head on the tile floor and saw stars. The energy ball hummed and pulsed a few inches above my face.

"Oh my gosh, are you okay?" Adele bent over to help me up.

"Why didn't you pass the ball?" Sasha asked.

"I guess I didn't move fast enough." I shrugged like I couldn't understand what happened either.

"I guess that's what happens when you spend all your time hanging around with humdrums. You start to suck at Spell-ball." Milo laughed and then poked Adele with his elbow. "That totally counts as a point for us. She missed the pass."

"It shouldn't count. Willow wasn't ready to play."

"She has twice the magical skills of the rest of us, and we don't say that's unfair," Milo pointed out, which just proved that he did think it was unfair.

"You're jealous," Sasha said.

"Jealous of having a humdrum know who I am? I don't think so. No way you'd catch me going to humdrum school." Milo crossed his arms over his chest.

"That's because you're too weird to fit in with humdrums." Sasha rolled her eyes at me. "Don't let him get to you, he wishes he could fly as good as you." Sasha and Adele stood next to me so that we were faced off against the boys. The Van Elder girls stood in the middle. They were totally boy crazy so I wasn't surprised they weren't going to pick our side.

"I fly plenty fast," Milo said.

Adele snorted. "You call that fast? I've seen fairies in their nineties fly faster than that and they were using walkers."

"Oh you think so? Fine. Let's have a race, Willow versus me. First one to the end of the hall and back wins."

"You're on! Prepare to eat her pixie dust, loser!" Sasha said.

My mind was spinning, how in the world was I going to explain my inability to fly? I waved my hand at Milo. "I don't want to embarrass you. Why don't you practice for a few weeks and then we'll race. I want to make sure you have a fair chance."

Adele laughed and gave me a high five.

"Whatever. We still get the point. You missed the ball, that means we score."

"Fine, you get the point. It still isn't going to help you." Adele rolled up her sleeves. "C'mon, Willow, you can play goal."

"Um. No thanks. You guys can play without me." I had no intention of getting hit by that ball again—it hurt.

"You have to play, you're the best in our class," Sasha said. Everyone started to take up their positions again. "I'll serve."

I swallowed. People might believe that I missed the ball once, but if I missed it again they were sure to guess there was something wrong. Spell-ball was a game that was supposed to help teach sprites to use magic and spells quickly. You used magic to pass the ball and get it into the other side's goal. You could use your natural ability, like floating, but there were extra points for using spells. You had to think on your feet.

The ball flew across the room, and I ducked. Jordan swooped in and took the ball.

"Eye on the ball, Doyle!" Fiona, one of the Van Elder twins, yelled. She hated to lose. It was safe to say good sportsmanship was not one of her special abilities.

I shot a quick look at the door. Where was Ms. Sullivan? There's never a teacher around when you want one, but if you're doing something you shouldn't be doing then they were always standing right behind you. I watched the ball as it bounced around the room.

"Head's up, Willow!" Sasha shot the ball in my direction. Uh-oh. I grabbed a book off the closest desk and used it like a racket to whack it back across the room.

"Hey! You can't use a book," Jordan said.

"Who said?" I demanded. "Besides, not using magic is like a humdrum spell."

"Yeah, not using magic should count for double points!" Sasha yelled.

"How do you figure?" Jordan said.

"Because it's harder to not use magic than to use it,"

Sasha said. "Duh. Would you want to face an energy ball without being able to do a spell?"

"Okay, all we need is one more point and we win," Adele pointed out. "Everyone take your mark."

If I lucked out one of the other girls would score before the ball came my way again. In fact, I could avoid the ball and say that I didn't want to hog the glory so that someone else could score the winning goal.

Fiona Van Elder stole the ball by using a flash glitter spell that momentarily blinded Milo. She reached, spun the ball around and looked who to pass it to for the point. I saw her eyes rest on me, and I opened my mouth to tell her to pass to her sister instead when there was a crash and a scream.

Ms. Sullivan was standing in the doorway. She'd dropped her giant tote bag and all her books spilled out onto the floor. Everyone froze in place, shocked. Ms. Sullivan never screamed. Not even when Milo accidentally spilled pixie dust on his lunch and his carrots attacked his cheese sandwich. Never give carrots toothpicks. They can be violent.

"Turn off that ball RIGHT NOW!"

Adele did a quick spell and the blue ball flickered for a moment and then disappeared.

"Do you realize what could have happened?" Ms. Sullivan said, looking around the room. "This is very dangerous."

All the other sprites were looking at each other in confusion. We'd been playing Spell-ball all year. I tried to motion to Ms. Sullivan so she would know to keep my secret, but she didn't notice.

"Without any magic, Willow could have been seriously injured. What if one of you had hit her in the face with the ball?"

The rest of the sprites turned to face me. Adele's mouth was hanging open.

"You don't have any magic?" Sasha asked shocked. "None? Like not even a small spell?"

"Not right now," I mumbled.

"Why didn't you say anything?" Fiona said.

I wondered if I could convince everyone that I'd simply forgotten to mention that I didn't have my abilities anymore. Like it was no big deal, so I had forgotten.

"I wouldn't tell anyone if I lost my magic either," Jordan said. "What I want to know is why you lost your abilities. You must have done something really wrong."

Ms. Sullivan clapped her hands together. "All right. Everyone take your seats. We have a lot to cover this afternoon. What Willow did is between her and the council that imposed the magical restriction."

We shuffled toward our desks.

"Geez, Willow, what did you do? Did you kill a humdrum by accident?" Jordan whispered as he moved past me to his seat.

"You could have told us," Adele said.

I didn't say anything. I slumped down in my chair and didn't look at anyone. I could tell my face was burning red hot from embarrassment.

Milo nudged me with his shoulder when he walked past my desk. "I knew I totally could beat you in a flying race. Who needs the flying practice now?"

I slumped down even farther. Milo was lucky I couldn't do any magic or he'd be sorry.

ten

If your annoying older sister has a boyfriend:

a. Being in love will make her happy.

b. She'll be so busy mooning over him that she'll leave you alone.

c. She'll start freaking out over every little thing.

Answer:

C. And, if possible, be even *more* annoying than she was before, especially because she'll start spending hours in the bathroom staring at herself, leaving you to pound on the door and have to beg to be let in.

"Are you going to wear that?" Lucinda asked, her nose wrinkling up when she saw my outfit.

I looked down. What did she expect me to wear? A

dress? We were eating at home. "What's wrong with what I'm wearing?"

Lucinda rolled her eyes. "If you don't know, then I don't know how to help you. Would it kill you to at least *try* to look nice?" She walked around our dining room table, lining up the silverware so that it was perfectly straight. Suddenly her eyes went wide and she lunged across the table to grab one of the glasses. "Mom! This one has a huge spot on it." She held it out. She looked horrified, like she had discovered a body in the front closet instead of a water spot.

"Let's not panic." Mom bustled in from the kitchen carrying a bowl of salad. She looked at the glass and gave a quick spell. There was a *plink* and the microscopic spot that freaked my sister out was gone.

Lucinda inspected the glass carefully. She'd invited Evan over for dinner, and the way she was acting, you would think Oberon, King of the Fairies, was going to come by. The house was so clean you could have eaten off the kitchen floor. If you looked too closely at the stove you would go blind from the glare off the polished surface. We had dinner every night. It wasn't like we were trying to do something really new and tricky, but Lucinda wasn't sure we could handle it.

I folded napkins to put at each place. Lucinda stood behind me supervising. I might only be ten, and not have any magical abilities, but I was perfectly capable of folding a napkin. I turned around and glared at her. "It's just a dinner, would you calm down?"

"Whatever you do, don't say anything to Evan about losing your magic." Lucinda refolded the napkin I'd just done. "I'd rather he didn't know. It's humiliating that someone in my family is in this situation."

"I wasn't planning on telling anyone," I said. I didn't mention what happened in spell class. There was a good chance Evan would have already heard about it from someone else. I was hoping that the Fairy Council would meet soon and rethink Miss Pipkins's decision. There was a time when I thought I didn't want to be magical, but I'd never wish for that again. I couldn't understand Winston anymore. I couldn't fly. I couldn't do even simple spells. I hated it.

"Maybe it would be better if you didn't say anything at all during dinner," Lucinda said. "Whatever you say will likely be wrong. Just sit there."

"Won't it seem weird if I don't talk?"

"Not as weird as whatever might come out of your mouth." Lucinda turned to my mom who was bringing in a basket of rolls. "And can you make sure Dad doesn't tell any of his jokes?"

This dinner was going to be great. We would all sit in total silence and watch Evan eat. The doorbell rang. "Hey, what's that thing on your nose?" I asked Lucinda, pointing at her face.

She rubbed her nose furiously. "What? Is there something there? What is it?" Her voice raised in panic. She rubbed her nose again. "Is it gone?"

"Nope. Still there." Her nose was actually completely clean, but I liked acting like there was a huge glob hanging off the end.

"Oh my gosh," Lucinda dashed out of the room to look at herself for the one millionth time while my dad answered the front door.

"Hey, Wills." Evan came into the dining room with my dad. He gave me one of his lazy smiles. Normally I hate when someone calls me Wills, but it sounded better when it came out of his mouth.

Lucinda came back into the room. The tip of her nose was bright red from where she had been rubbing it. She shot me a look that let me know she was now aware there had never been anything on her face.

I pulled out my chair to sit down, but Lucinda yanked

it out of my hand. "Evan's our guest. He'll sit here. You can sit over there." She pointed at the extra chair my dad had squished to fit around the table. I was going to have to eat in the corner where I would bump elbows with my mom and dad the entire time. Just so she could sit right next to Evan.

"Here, let me," Evan pulled out the chair for my sister.

I plopped down in the corner chair and whacked my knee against the table leg. My dad held the chair for my mom. All of a sudden our dinners were formal. The only thing we were missing was a butler. My mom said a quiet spell and suddenly each of us had a pile of pasta on our plates. Cheese and a small grater came floating out of the kitchen and hovered above each plate, waiting for us to nod before sprinkling a small shower of parmesan onto the pasta below.

"This cheese reminds me of a joke," my dad said, but before he could share it he winced. My mom had kicked him under the table. "All right, I forgot, but it was a funny joke." He rubbed his knee.

"So, Evan, are you and your family planning any vacations this year?" my mom asked, saving us from having to eat in silence except for the sound of people slurping their noodles.

"We're going to Paris in the spring," Evan said. "We go every few years because my mom does a lot of fashion wishes."

"I've always thought Paris was the most romantic city," Lucinda gushed. "I think it would be nice to live there for a few years after school."

I paused with the fork halfway to my mouth. Really? This was the first time I'd ever heard my sister talk about moving to Paris. I suspected if Evan told us how they were going to visit the Yukon, my sister would suddenly talk about how she always loved cold weather and polar bears.

"So, Wills, how are things with your humdrum friend?" Evan asked.

I opened my mouth, but Lucinda cut me off before I could get the first word out. "Her friend is fine. Nothing going on there. No news." Lucinda glared at me across the table like I had done something wrong. *He* was the one who had asked *me* a question. I could have said something. It wasn't like I was going to tell him about losing my magic. I had *some* social skills.

"Tell us more about Paris," Lucinda said. She had a piece of parsley stuck in between her front teeth, but there was no way I was going to tell her. She could have had a whole tree branch stuck there and I wouldn't have said a word. After all, I wasn't supposed to talk.

"Paris is boring compared to what's going on with you guys. I still can't get over the fact that after hundreds—thousands—of years, the barrier between fairies and humdrums has been broken down." Evan was practically bouncing in his seat he was so excited. I could tell he was really interested, too, not just being polite. "And who would have guessed that if it was going to happen, it would happen this way. You'd think it would have been something more formal, like the president of the United States having a summit with the Fairy Council or something." Evan raised his water glass to me. "You lucked out with getting such a cool sister," he said to Lucinda.

I tapped his water glass back to complete the toast. "She *is* pretty lucky, isn't she? Some sisters wouldn't appreciate how lucky they were. They might be the kind who would be mean to their little sisters," I said with a smile.

"We're so close, we're like best friends and sisters rolled into one," Lucinda said, giving me a huge fake smile back and rushing to clink glasses with the both of us.

"We sure are. Why, if we weren't so close, then Lucinda wouldn't let me borrow her purple sweater tomorrow," I said.

Lucinda's eyes narrowed. She never let me borrow her clothes because she said I would spill things on them. She's right about me being kind of messy, but it isn't like the sweater couldn't be washed. I knew there would be no way she would turn me down now, with Evan listening. "Of course you can borrow it," she said through her teeth. "What are sisters for?"

"I think it's cool you guys get along. I've always wanted a kid sister," Evan said. "I have an older brother, but he teased me all the time. He was terrible to me growing up. You wouldn't believe the stuff he used to do to me."

"I'd believe it," I said, giving him a sympathetic smile. "I hear stories about what older siblings can be like. It's a tragedy." I knew I liked Evan. He understood what it was like to be tortured by a cruel sibling. No wonder he had such nice eyes. He'd known real pain.

"We should all go out together. I'd love to talk more to your friend Katie," Evan said. "I've never really spent any time with a humdrum. I'd love to know what she thinks about stuff. We could all get ice cream sometime."

"Willow hates ice cream," Lucinda said.

I laughed. "She's teasing you. I love ice cream. So does Katie. We'd love to go out with you guys. It'll be fun."

Lucinda's mouth was in a thin line. "Yeah. Lots of fun." I couldn't tell what she thought was worse, that she was now going to have to be nice to me because otherwise I might tell Evan, or that she was going to have to hang out with me and Katie.

"That's great!" Evan looked really excited. It could hardly be considered my fault that Evan would rather spend time with Katie and me than alone with my sister. Most likely it was because I had such a good sense of humor. Lucinda was too serious all the time. Evan looked like the kind of guy who liked to have fun.

Lucinda snapped her fingers. "Darn it, I just thought of something. Willow and her friend Katie are so busy these days with their humdrum science fair. They probably don't have a lot of time to go out for silly things like ice cream with us." She shook her head sadly as if she had gotten really bad news. "And I was really looking forward to it too. Of course I understand you guys need to focus on the science fair. After all, didn't you say it was super important that your humdrum friend won?"

"Katie plans to be an astronaut," I explained to Evan.

"The winner of the science fair gets to go to NASA Camp Kennedy Space Center. That would be pretty much a dream come true for her."

Evan looked thrilled. "That's great. It's like a wish of hers. We should grant it."

"NO!" my parents yelled out at the same time. Evan looked shocked. Mom smoothed down her skirt. "What we mean is that the Fairy Council has indicated it would be better if we didn't do any magic to help Willow's friend right now. They want to make sure that the fact that they're friends doesn't make things unfair. We shouldn't grant wishes for a humdrum simply because we like them." Mom smiled at everyone around the table. "Would anyone like more salad?"

"If we can't grant her wish, then we should be there to support her," Evan said. "The council can't have a problem with us cheering her on. That's what friends do for one another." He smiled at Lucinda, proud of himself for solving the problem.

I could tell Lucinda wasn't happy about the idea at all, but she couldn't let Evan know that she was actually evil and mean. She wanted him to think she was sweet and nice. Sooner or later the poor guy was going to figure it out, but I couldn't blame my sister for trying to keep it a secret. Everyone has secrets. I couldn't do magic, my dad was bad at telling jokes, Winston liked to eat shoes, and our whole family had a gnome problem.

No one had seen Jakob, the science-fair-project-ruining garden gnome, for days. My dad had left a formal note in our greenhouse requesting a meeting. The note disappeared, but he didn't write back. I thought that was rude, but I guess if someone will ruin a kid's science project we shouldn't be surprised if he doesn't have the best manners. My parents were sure that Jakob was still hanging out in the greenhouse, but that he would likely leave me alone now. I hoped they were right, but you never know with gnomes.

eleven

True or False:

You shouldn't assume that just because someone once stole your notebook, threw French fries at you, shot his imaginary laser gun at you, and partnered with your enemy for the science fair, that he's a bad person.

Answer:

True. It might turn out that the fry thrower can be a bit of a hero. (Even if he is still sort of dorky about quoting from stupid space movies.)

Ms. Caul drove the four of us to the science center where the state competition was being held, so we didn't have to carry our projects over. It was pretty special because we got to get out of school. The rest of our class was stuck with Ms. Kysell as a substitute. No one liked Ms. Kysell. She was pretty old, but dyed her hair bright red. Her mouth always had a wide smile, but the smile didn't reach as far as her eyes. She had eyes like a hawk. She was one of those people who acted like she was being very nice and wanted to be friendly, but in reality she was just hoping to catch you doing something wrong. I was much happier to spend the afternoon with Ms. Caul.

"Will there be a plug near our table?" Bethany asked from the backseat of the van. "I have to be able to plug our heart in so the judges can see it beating."

"You've already asked about the plug a hundred million times," Katie pointed out.

"That's okay. It's easy to forget when you're nervous," Ms. Caul said from the front. "There'll be a plug. I made sure to tell the organizer you needed one."

"Think how nervous she would be if she actually made the project herself," I whispered to Katie, who giggled.

Bethany snatched a pen out of Nathan's hand. He'd been using it like a drumstick on his leg. "Be careful. What are you going to do if you get ink all over your outfit?"

Nathan rolled his eyes. He and Bethany had both dressed up today. It didn't make any sense to me. All we were doing was setting up our projects. We wouldn't even meet the judges until tomorrow. Bethany insisted that you could only make a first impression once, and you never knew if the judges might stop by. She was wearing a skirt and she'd made Nathan wear dress pants. She wanted him to wear a tie, but he refused.

My mouth went dry when we pulled up in front of the science center. The building was huge. It was the size of a football stadium and right inside the front door I could see a giant dinosaur skeleton. Groups of kids buzzed in and out of the building like bees. I didn't know there were this many kids in the entire state, let alone this many who were interested in science. The four of us stood on the steps watching the van while Ms. Caul went to get a cart for our projects.

"Did you see that?" Katie whispered to me as some older kids, at least seventh graders, carried a giant mechanical arm past us. "The competition is going to be really stiff. I heard that there's a private school downstate that hires professors from the university to come and help their students with their projects. Professional scientists." Katie shook her head like she couldn't even imagine it.

Bethany tossed her hair over her shoulder. "I don't think we have anything to worry about. Our project has everything it needs to win." She looked at my plants sitting on the sidewalk. "Look at the bright side, Willow, you didn't stand a chance anyway so you don't need to worry."

I probably didn't stand a chance. I wouldn't have been here at all except for the fact that Jakob had done something to my project and turned them into some kind of freakish superplants. Even if I wasn't going to win, I didn't like Bethany pointing it out. I turned my back to ignore her.

"What's with you and your family and plants, anyway?" Bethany snorted. "Have you seen the front yard of their house?" she asked Nathan. "It's the weirdest thing. People all over town talk about it."

"What's wrong with our yard?" I put my hands on my hips.

Katie stood at my side so we were both faced off with Bethany. "I think it's cool," Katie said.

"Figures you would like it. No wonder you two are friends. You're as freaky as her and her family." Bethany tossed her hair again. "If you looked up freaks in the dictionary they would have a picture of the two of you. You could have studied each other for the science fair, at least it would have been more interesting than what you did."

"Who are you calling freaks?" I crossed my arms over my chest. I might make fun of my family, but it was *my* family. I was the only one allowed to do it. And making fun of my best friend? Not cool.

"I bet your freaky dad is the one who did your project for you anyway. He probably just dug something out of your front yard." She laughed and nudged Nathan, but he took a step away from her.

"I think Willow's project is cool. You should leave it alone," Nathan said. "Besides, the last thing you should talk about is cheating."

Bethany's entire face turned bright red. It was like she was turning into a tomato. "I-I . . . don't know what you're talking about," she sputtered.

"I'm talking about the fact that your dad made our whole project. Well, except for the labels, your mom made those. We didn't do a darn thing."

Katie and I looked at each other in shock. Nathan was now standing on our side, and Bethany was next to their plastic heart by herself.

"They didn't do the project, they just helped!"

Bethany insisted. "If you weren't happy with the project then you should have said something."

"I'm saying it now. I'm going to tell Ms. Caul to take my name off the project."

"You can't do that!" Bethany screeched. "Not now!"

"I don't cheat at sports, and I don't cheat in science," Nathan said, his voice firm.

All of us stood in a circle staring at each other. "Fine. I'll tell Ms. Caul to take your name off and when I win— and I *will* win—then I'll go to space camp without you. I hope you know this means you're never going to be a space smuggler." Bethany stomped toward the door to find Ms. Caul.

"Wow," Katie said, watching her storm off.

"Thanks for sticking up for me," I said. I picked at the leaves on one of the plants.

Nathan shrugged. "Sure. And you should ignore what Bethany said about your dad. I think your yard is cool. I liked when he did the dragon thing."

"Gardening is sort of his hobby."

"You should see if he could do a *Space Fighter*-themed yard some time." Nathan crouched down and pretended to shoot people as they came in and out of the science center. "He could make a giant evergreen blaster and then a bunch of purple-laser flowers shooting out."

"Um, sure. I'll tell him about that idea." I thought that was a pretty stupid plan, but I wouldn't tell him that after he had been so nice to me.

Boys can be weird, but you sort of have to put up with those parts if you like the rest of them. They come as a package. You just have to decide if the parts that drove you crazy outweighed the good parts. I was going to write that down in my notebook when I had a chance. I was going to do it in secret, though, just in case Nathan tried to steal it.

twelve

True or False:

Everything that could go wrong has already gone wrong.

Answer:

False. You won't even be able to imagine how many MORE wrong things can happen.

I walked to the science center. My parents were coming later with Evan and Lucinda to cheer Katie and me on. Lucinda even made signs last night that said: GO WILLOW and KATIE = SCIENCE GENIUS! She outlined our names with glue and glitter. I thought the signs were a bit much, but ever since Evan had come over for dinner she was being superfriendly to me. It made me nervous, sort of like having a cobra as a friend. I reached into my pocket and felt Winston's disgusting toy hot dog. It was his favorite. He'd given it to me this morning for good luck. At least, I'm pretty sure that was what he was trying to communicate. He also might have been trying to tell me he wanted a hot dog. I really hoped the Fairy Council would give me my powers back soon. I missed being able to talk to Winston. He usually didn't have good advice, but it was nice to hear his opinion.

I hadn't even walked all the way up the stairs to the giant auditorium when Katie tackled me.

"OH MY GOSH. You have to come quick." Katie grabbed me by the elbow and dragged me toward the room.

"What's the matter?" I said.

Katie stopped and lowered her voice so only I could hear her. "We've got a major gnome issue on our hands."

My heart stopped. Uh-oh. "Is it bad?"

"I don't even have the words to describe it," Katie said. She pointed and I could see there was a crowd gathered in the far corner of the auditorium where our projects were set up. "Bethany is going to have a cow when she sees this."

"Bethany? Is her project damaged too?" Jakob must

really be angry. I wished my parents had stayed with me instead of dropping me off. I was scared enough that I even wished my sister was here.

"You have to see it for yourself," Katie pulled me along until we were standing at the edge of the crowd. People were pushing and clustered into a tight knot. We had to squeeze ourselves in so we could get to the front. My mouth fell open when I saw our projects.

Bethany's heart project was on its side and spewing fake blood up into the air. It looked like a fountain in the center of a mall. People could have thrown coins in to make a wish—that one of us fairies would then have to answer. Nathan was standing near the project looking shocked. He was holding one of the plastic arteries that must have broken off the side. He had the red-dyed water splashed all over his shirt.

Katie nudged me with her elbow and pointed to her project. Her robotic rover was in the aisle. At first I didn't think anything was wrong. It was running back and forth like it was supposed to. Then suddenly the engine revved and it flipped over, tilted on its side, and did a row of cartwheels down the aisle. Her robot was doing gymnastics. I swallowed. I was pretty sure it wasn't supposed to do that.

"How is it doing that?" I whispered.

"I have no idea. I have the remote in my pocket. There aren't even any batteries in it yet. I took the batteries home to recharge them last night." Katie said. She held out her hand to show me a pile of batteries. I wasn't a super science whiz, but I knew batteries were required for these kinds of things. This meant the only option left was magic. Katie was right. We had a gnome problem.

"I guess we should consider ourselves lucky that it isn't running anyone over," I said, trying to find the positive in the situation. "We'll have to come up with some way to explain what happened. Can you say it has crossed wires or something?"

"I can try, but I don't have any way to turn it off." Katie turned around to face me. "The real question is what do we say about your project?"

I'd forgotten about my project. What else could Jakob do to it? I would have noticed when I came in if the plants had grown through the roof. Then I saw my plants. My mind went as blank as a fresh sheet of construction paper. There wasn't going to be any way to explain this.

The plants had grown bright rainbow-colored leaves, striped red, purple, blue, and green. The stems had small polka dots all over them. In the center of the leaves there was something growing, almost like a flower. I took a step closer to see what it was. My heart beat even faster. My plant was growing Barbie dolls. Barbie in a swimsuit, Malibu Barbie, Sporty Barbie, Black Barbie, Barbie in an evening gown, Vintage Barbie, even a few of Barbie's friends were scattered here and there. I saw at least one Ken doll and a couple Skippers tucked into the smaller leaves. I had a bunch of wild Mattel plants on my hands.

"Can you fix it?" Katie asked.

"I don't have any magic." I threw up my hands in frustration. "I can't do a single spell. My grandma has a meeting, and I don't know how to reach my parents."

Katie grabbed both of my hands so she could stare into my eyes. "Don't panic. You don't need your parents to help. You don't need magic. We can figure this out."

I'd always relied on magic to fix my problems, from saving my sister from a fairy-eating lizard, to giving Bethany the hiccups. When I didn't have magic, then my parents or Grandma had always been there to help. It made me nervous to think about doing this on my own. I made myself take a deep breath.

"We need to capture Jakob. He's the one who did this, so he should be able to undo it," I said.

EILEEN COOK

"Okay, good. That's where we'll start. How do you capture a gnome?" Katie asked.

My mind raced. "I don't know. I knew I should've read the whole fairy handbook . . .

"First, we have to find him. He might be hiding in my dad's greenhouse. He would have to be near our science projects to do the magic, and with his stubby legs he wouldn't be able to walk too far so I don't think he's moved away."

"Okay, you need to get him, and I'll try and figure out some way to deflect attention around here."

"Hey, how did you get it to grow like that?" Nathan asked, interrupting us. Katie and I jumped apart. I hoped he hadn't heard what we were talking about.

"Uh . . ." I wasn't sure what to say. "It's sort of complicated."

"I notice things have a way of getting complicated when you're around," Nathan said with a smile. "I'm not saying it's a bad thing, but it is sort of noticeable."

There was a noise as someone shoved their way through the crowd. Bethany rushed toward us. Her mouth was pulled up in a snarl and she looked mad enough to spit nails. Miranda and Paula were trailing behind her.

"You did this!" Bethany yelled, as she got closer. "You ruined my project because you wanted to win."

"I promise I didn't touch your project." I turned to Katie and whispered, "I need to find Jakob right now."

"This is so cool," Paula said, as she walked up to the table. She harvested a Barbie off one of my plants. "Can you grow new outfits, too? I always wanted the Cher Barbie when I was a kid."

Bethany whacked the doll out of Paula's hands. "Will you focus on what's important!"

"I can't stay. I have to go." I took a few steps back. When the Fairy Council saw what happened, Miss Pipkins was really going to be mad. Maybe now she would realize Jakob was the real trouble, not me.

"You're not going anywhere until I get an explanation," Bethany demanded.

"Calm down, Bethany," Miranda said. She patted her softly on the back. It was like trying to calm a rabid dog by rubbing his ears. Normally Bethany would do anything Miranda asked, she was a total kiss-up. Maybe it was because she thought her dad would be mad about the plastic heart, or because Nathan had refused to stay her project partner, or maybe she had finally reached a point where she was going to snap, but there was no way she was giving up.

"I really need to go. I'll come back and then I'm sure I can explain everything."

Bethany lunged for me. I was pretty sure she was going to throw me to the floor and lie on top of me like a World Wide Wrestling star until the police were called.

Katie and Nathan moved together at the same time, blocking Bethany. They were like my own personal bodyguards.

"Run for it, Willow!" Nathan yelled.

I hesitated for a second, but then I took off. I wove through the crowd, dodging and diving until I was out of the room. I could hear Bethany yelling something behind me, but I didn't stop.

I kept running right outside the building and down the steps. Katie would do what she could to fix the situation at the science center, but I had to fix the gnome problem myself and I had to do it the humdrum way. No magic allowed.

thirteen

If you need to capture a rogue garden gnome you should try:

a. traps

b. tricks

c. bait (rumor has it they have a weakness for peanut butter)

d. giant flypaper

e. begging

f. Do you have any ideas to add here?

Answer:

Anything and everything you can think of!

I ran into the house screaming for my parents, but no one was home. I grabbed the holo-phone and called my grandma. The holo-phone would let me see my grandma while we talked and seeing her would make me feel better. Hugging her would be even better, but I didn't have time to get over to her house. I knew she was meeting with the Fairy Council this morning, but I was hoping to catch her before she left. No answer. I was on my own.

Well, maybe not completely on my own. Winston came down the stairs yawning. He looked at me and then at the clock on the mantle. His head cocked to one side in confusion. I could tell he was wondering what I was doing back from the science fair so early. Not to mention I was all sweaty from my run back here to the house.

"Gnomes," I explained.

Winston harrumphed and looked down his muzzle at me with his eyebrows raised.

"I know! I underestimated how much trouble someone who was small could cause. You'd think I would have known better since I've seen what you can do. He ruined our science projects again, and not just a little. He's made a huge mess of everything."

Winston growled. His tail stuck straight out behind him.

I took that to mean he didn't like Jakob any better

than I did. "I have to find a way to catch him and make him fix the mess at the science center. My dad said he'd seen signs that he was still hanging out in the greenhouse. I have to figure out how to catch him without using any magic. There's no way he's going to surrender, and the only way I can think of to catch him is to use a mousetrap, but I'm pretty sure if I capture him with that it's going to really hurt."

Winston gave an excited bark and ran toward the kitchen. I rushed after him. He ran to the cupboard where my mom kept his dog biscuits. I put my hands on my hips. Did he always have to think with his stomach?

"Winston, this is not the time for a snack. Have you been listening to anything I've said? I need to come up with a plan."

Winston gave an annoyed-sounding *woof.* He ran over to another cupboard, jumping up and barking. I opened the cupboard. It's where my mom kept things like bags of rice, noodles, and a giant jar of peanut butter. When my hand skimmed over the peanut butter jar, Winston went nuts. He spun in circles.

"What? You like peanut butter now?"

Winston ran back to the dog biscuit cupboard and

then back to me with the peanut butter jar. He spun back and forth between the two, faster and faster.

"I don't understand what you're trying to say," I said.

Winston jumped up to the windowsill and snatched my mom's potted basil plant and carried it over in his mouth. He shook the plant in front of the peanut butter jar. He dropped the plant and then licked his lips over and over.

What he was trying to say suddenly clicked into place. "Gnomes love peanut butter? Are you sure?" Winston spun in circles in excitement, which I took to mean he was certain. I wasn't sure how he knew what gnomes liked, but he was the kind of dog who always surprised me with the random trivia he knew. He would be a big winner on *Jeopardy*, if people could understand what he was saying. And as long as he didn't bite Alex Trebek. "You think we should use this as bait?"

Winston was so happy I'd figured out what he was saying that he rolled around on the floor with his feet in the air. He jumped up and crouched down. He acted like he was sneaking up on someone and then he pounced.

"It's a plan. We'll use the peanut butter as bait, and when he comes out, you'll help me capture him. This is way better than a mousetrap." I leaned down and stared into Winston's eyes. "Absolutely no biting allowed. I need to convince Jakob to fix things. If you bite him, he isn't going to be very interested in helping me out."

Winston snorted, the fur around his muzzle blowing out.

"If he doesn't offer to help, then you can bite him, okay?" I made a quick mental list of what I would need and gathered them up quickly and ran out to the greenhouse. I pushed the door slowly open and looked around. There were still some piles of dirt on the floor. My heart sped up when I saw a tiny footprint in one of the piles. Winston waited outside, crouched down and ready to pounce. I opened the peanut butter jar, put it in the middle of the floor, and sat down on the bench.

"Are you in here, Jakob?" I called out. I listened, but it was quiet. I could smell the peanut butter, and I hoped that his little gnome nose was twitching. "I need to talk to you."

An empty clay pot on the ground tipped over, clattering on the cement floor. He was here.

"I have some questions about, um, some plants." I hoped he wouldn't guess my questions were nothing more than a trap. "You don't have to worry. I'll stay over here."

There was a rustle and scraping sound from under

the table. Jakob pulled himself out. He slid closer to the peanut butter, keeping his back pressed against the table, staying far out of my reach.

"Are you still mad about the science plants?" Jakob's eyes shot back and forth between the jar of peanut butter and me.

"What you did wasn't very nice," I said.

"I tried to talk about it nicely, but you wouldn't listen. I had to teach you a lesson."

"Here, I brought you this as a peace offering." I pulled a teaspoon out of my pocket and held it out to him. I could see he was torn between his overwhelming desire for peanut butter and his distrust of me.

Jakob inched forward, stretching as far as he could until he snatched the spoon from my hand and scurried back out of my reach. When I didn't move he relaxed and plunked himself down on the floor, pulling the jar of peanut butter closer so that it was propped up between his legs.

"Now, this is much more civilized." He dug the spoon into the peanut butter. "You said you had a question about plants? The secret is respect. You should treat a plant the way you would treat a good friend." Jakob opened his mouth wide to shove the peanut butter in.

"I wouldn't call having a plant growing Barbie dolls very respectful," I pointed out.

Jakob looked at me with his bushy eyebrows raised. "Humprph?" His mouth was glued shut with peanut butter. He looked confused.

Winston burst through the door and gave an excited bark before leaping into the air and throwing himself at Jakob with a ninja-style attack. Or at least the best job a small dog can do to imitate a ninja. Jakob and Winston rolled around on the floor. They bumped into the potting table and knocked three plants off. The pots exploded when they hit the floor and dirt went everywhere. I jumped up from the bench and shoved my empty school backpack over Jakob.

"Sit on him!" I yelled. Winston plunked his furry butt down on the wriggling bag so that I could pull out the duct tape. I taped all around the bag with only Jakob's head sticking out the top.

I sat back sweating from all the effort. Winston was covered in dirt from the floor and peanut butter. Jakob looked extremely upset. He had a smear of peanut butter on his cheek. His hat had been knocked off during the struggle. I leaned over and placed it back onto his head. It fell over one of his eyes.

"This is gnome-napping!" Jakob yelled. He wriggled in the bag. "I'm going to the Fairy Council to complain. Attack on a magical creature is going to put you in a lot of trouble."

"You have a no business complaining to the council after what you did. That kind of flashy magic could get the attention of humdrums. Barbie dolls growing on trees? Heart fountains? Cartwheeling robots? You don't get any more flashy than what you did. The only reason I'm kidnapping you is to make you go back and fix it. The council will probably give me a medal for this." I didn't mention that I didn't want a medal. What I wanted was my magic back and for Katie to win the science fair.

"I don't know what you're talking about!" Jakob huffed. "Gnomes are restricted to natural magic. I wouldn't have the first idea how to make a robot, and even if I did know how, I don't have the slightest interest."

I crossed my arms over my chest. "Oh, really? Then how come you admitted just a moment ago that you had to teach me a lesson? I heard you, and Winston was a witness." I was proud of myself. I was like Sherlock Holmes. There was no way he could deny it.

"I did mess with your plants last week. That's what I meant about teaching you a lesson. I touched only your project. The growth was a bit much, but it wouldn't be anything that couldn't be explained away to the hum-drums," Jakob said.

My stomach started to tie itself back into a knot. Jakob seemed pretty sure of himself. I'd expected him to break down and admit to everything. "But if you didn't cause the trouble today, who did?"

"I haven't the slightest idea," Jakob said. I was trying to figure out what to do next when I heard voices in the yard. "Help! Help!" Jakob yelled out the open green-house door. "I've been attacked by a sprite!"

"Shh!" I lunged to the floor to cover Jakob's mouth with my hand. Before I could hush him up the green-house door flew open and my grandma was standing there with Miss Pipkins.

Uh-oh. I had an angry gnome duct-taped into my backpack, dirt all over my dad's greenhouse, a dog smeared with peanut butter, and the science fair was still ruined.

Miss Pipkins' mouth was hanging wide open and she was blinking like she couldn't believe what she was seeing. I couldn't really blame her.

"I . . . I . . . I . . . can explain," I stammered.

"Really? I'd like to hear this," Jakob said.

I opened my mouth, but nothing came out. Winston whined and his tail drooped to the floor. Grandma had her hand over her mouth. I sighed. There was no way to explain this. I was never going to get my magic back.

fourteen

True or False:
Sometimes when everything has gone wrong it is because someone was trying to make everything go right.

Answer:
True.

I sat on the living room sofa with my head down. I could never figure out how I always managed to end up in trouble for just trying to do the right thing. I was a bad luck magnet.

Jakob was sitting on a kitchen chair with his feet hanging off, enjoying the peanut butter sandwich my grandma made him. "Don't think this will change my mind. I still plan to press charges." He pointed at Winston. "And I want the dog in trouble too. Someone should whack him with a rolled-up newspaper." He chewed with his mouth open, making loud peanut butter–smacking noises. In addition to being mean, gnomes have no table manners. Yet another reason no one invites them over for dinner. Grandma inched away from him, and I remembered that she didn't like gnomes either.

Miss Pipkins stood near the door wringing her hands. "I can't believe this. First she's doing magic against orders, and now she has a gnome shoved in a bag."

"I know you were upset about what happened last week, " Grandma said.

I sighed. "This isn't about last week,"—I shot a look at Jakob—"although I still think what he did then was lousy. I was trying to capture Jakob because something new has happened." I chewed on my thumbnail. "Only, now I'm not sure he's the one who ruined everything."

"What's ruined?" Lucinda came in the door with Evan trailing behind her. "We're just headed over to the science center. Mom and Dad are running late and told us to go ahead without them. We came to get the signs to cheer you guys on." She started to hold up the GO

WILLOW sign, but then saw how serious everyone looked.

Evan looked around the room. "Is everything okay?"

"That sprite used her attack dog to assault me!" Jakob said. He wiped his hands on his wool pants. "I could use another peanut butter sandwich. Chunky this time. I find peanut butter very soothing."

"You attacked a gnome?" Lucinda dropped the sign with my name on it. She shot a look at Evan to see what he thought of the situation.

"I thought he was the one who went crazy with the magic at the science center and ruined everything," I explained.

Lucinda's face went pale. It looked like she was going to pass out. I was surprised that she cared that much. "What do you mean 'ruin'?" she said in a whispery voice.

"That's what I keep trying to explain to everyone! I went to the science center today and everything has gone haywire. My plants are polka-dotted, and Katie's rover is jumping all around."

"But if Jakob isn't responsible, then who did it?" Miss Pipkins said.

"Well, I can tell you it wasn't a gnome. You wouldn't see a gnome adding *plastic* to a plant," Jakob said.

"But it's obviously someone with magic, and for once it can't be this sprite. I took her magic away myself," Miss Pipkins pointed out.

Finally everyone was paying attention to the important thing instead of worrying about an annoying gnome who had by now already eaten his second peanut butter sandwich.

"Lucinda? What do you know about this?" Grandma asked.

All of us turned to face Lucinda who was still really pale. As soon as Grandma asked her, she started to shake.

"You? You ruined our projects?" I was shocked. Even Evan looked surprised. I could have told him she was evil, but even I didn't think she would stoop this low.

"I was trying to help!" Lucinda wailed.

"Making my plant have polka dots isn't helping," I pointed out.

"There weren't supposed to be polka dots. I don't know what happened with Katie's either. I used an improvement spell. It was supposed to make your projects just that extra bit better. I wanted Katie to win. I've done that spell lots of times. I don't know why it went wrong."

It figures the one time my perfect sister gets something wrong it's a spell she does for me.

"I think it's awesome you would do that for your sister and her friend," Evan said. Lucinda threw herself into his arms, and he hugged her.

"You know I would do anything for my sister," Lucinda said, looking up at him with a smile.

Ah. The mystery of why my sister wanted to help me was solved. She wanted Evan's attention. And even though she ended up screwing everything up, she got it.

"Is there no one in this family who understands they aren't supposed to do magic for the humdrum?" Miss Pipkins rolled her eyes. "I'm going to have to take this to the Fairy Council." She shook her finger in Lucinda's face. "When you realize how much trouble you're going to be in, it will take the smile off your face."

"We can decide how to deal with Lucinda later. First we need to fix what's happened. I think I know why the spell went so wrong," Grandma said. "Magical overload. Jakob had already enchanted the projects last week. When Lucinda did her spell it was simply too much magic in one small place. It could have been worse, I suppose: It could have blown up."

"Blow up? Our projects are still in the middle of the

science center. Katie's back there trying to keep things calm until I could bring Jakob back and make him fix everything."

"Oh, good heavens. We better get over there." Miss Pipkins gathered up her things. "How in the world we're going to fix this, I have no idea."

"We might need Jakob to undo his original spell," Grandma said.

"I'm not going anywhere," Jakob said. "I've had enough of fairies to last me a lifetime."

"Too bad," Evan swept Jakob up in his arms and stuck him in the backpack. He slung the bag over his shoulder. "Let's go."

All of us ran out of the door. There was a science fair to be saved.

fifteen

If you have a really big problem, to fix it you will need:
  a. at least four fairy godmothers, a gnome, and one fighting ninja dog
  b. Level 7 spell magic
  c. one clear-thinking best friend

Answer:
  C.

"Try and blend in," Grandma said as we walked into the auditorium for the science fair. It might be a bit difficult for us to look normal. Evan was holding hands with Lucinda and they still had Jakob in the backpack with just the tip of his red hat sticking out. I had Winston tucked under my arm, and his fur still had clumps of peanut butter in it. I led everyone through the crowd to where our projects were set up.

My plant looked exactly the way I remembered it. I heard Miss Pipkins take a deep breath when she saw it. Nathan and Bethany's heart must have finally run out of dyed water because it wasn't spraying water anymore. The pieces were piled on an empty table. Then I saw Katie. She was sitting on top of her robot rover. When she saw me she smiled and waved. When she saw I had Evan with me, she reached up and patted her hair into place.

"Are you okay?" I asked as soon as I got closer.

"Sort of, I can't get up or else the robot starts flipping around all over again. I'm the only thing keeping it in place." Katie leaned forward and we could see the robot's wheels starting to spin until she put her weight back down.

"It'll be okay. I brought some help." I motioned to Grandma and Miss Pipkins. I put Winston down so he could sniff around.

"I can't do any magic unless you give me my powers back," Grandma said to Miss Pipkins. She looked around the room to make sure no one was paying attention to us. "Unless you want to take care of this yourself."

Miss Pipkins jumped. "Me?" she squeaked. "I don't think . . . I mean, I don't . . ." She wrung her hands. "Maybe it would be best if you did it." She rummaged through her bag and pulled out her badge, flipping it quickly at my grandma. "Under Section 14.5.3, your powers are now officially reinstated."

Grandma stumbled back and then stood up straight. She raised her arms above her head and wriggled her fingers. "Oooh, that feels ever so much better." She stretched her neck to each side. "Okay, let's start with getting this robot under control. " She said a quick spell under her breath and the robot Katie was sitting on suddenly went still.

"Whew." Katie stood slowly. "I was afraid I'd have to sit on that robot forever."

Grandma looked around the room. "Okay, now we need to figure out what to do next. Too much time has gone by to do a forget-me-spell."

"What about a distraction spell?" Lucinda suggested.

"With a crowd this large?" Miss Pipkins looked around the room. "I'm not sure it would work."

I tried to think of a spell option, but so far my Saturday spell classes had focused on easier projects. This kind of situation was going to call for some heavy-duty spell magic. Way above my sprite level.

"We could do a sleep spell and then sneak these projects out," Evan offered.

"That's brilliant," Lucinda gushed. Evan blushed and shrugged.

"You don't have to do anything. Nathan and I took care of it," Katie said, interrupting our list of ideas.

Everyone turned to look at Katie, surprised.

"You took care of it?" Miss Pipkins said. She looked at Katie, shocked. "Whatever did you do? You don't have any magic, you're a humdrum. How in the world . . ."

"We didn't use magic. We told the science fair organizers that we had messed with our own projects because we wanted to win. We said we wanted to win so bad that we tried to make our projects look better than they really were."

I sucked in my breath, shocked. "You told them you cheated?"

"And they believed"—Grandma waved her hands in front of our projects—"that all of this was something you did?"

Katie shrugged. "Sure. What else would they believe? There's no way they would believe it was a crazed robot. That seems too weird. Most people don't believe in magic, even when it's right in front of them."

"Amazing," Evan said. "She fixed it without magic. You're quite a humdrum."

Katie blushed. "I didn't do it by myself. Nathan helped."

Miss Pipkins smacked her forehead. "Another humdrum knows about us? I knew this would happen. It's just a matter of time until we're on CNN."

"Nathan doesn't know about you or magic. He just thinks Willow is sort of weird and needed some help," Katie explained. Lucinda gave one of her snorts, which showed she thought Nathan was right about me being odd.

"Great," I said.

"He thinks you're weird in a good way," Katie explained.

I wasn't sure there was a good way to be weird, but I guess it was nice that he helped Katie cover up for my problem. Suddenly something awful occurred to me. "If you and Nathan told the organizers you cheated, then this means you can't win!"

Katie swallowed and looked away. "They disqualified us. A sixth-grader won for his project on electricity. They announced it a few minutes ago. It's okay. I know I did a good job on my project. My mom always says trying your best is what's important."

"But what about space camp?" I asked.

Katie shrugged and I could tell she wasn't talking because she didn't want to cry. Winston leaned his body against her leg and she rubbed his ears. Dogs can make anyone feel better.

"You gave up your dream to help Willow?" Miss Pipkins asked softly. "I was told winning was one of your greatest wishes."

"What's a wish compared to a friend?" Katie threw her arm around me. "I can keep wishing, but Willow needed my help now."

"A humdrum helping a fairy godmother." Miss Pipkins sounded shocked.

"Well, it looks as if things have turned out all right in the end." Grandma looked around the room and saw people packing up their projects. "We should get these projects in the car before anyone looks too closely at them."

There was a rustle in Evan's backpack. "Will you turn around once in a while? I can't see a thing back here."

"Oops, sorry," Evan spun around so Jakob could see.

"Look at that plant," he moaned. "How you can say things are all right? It has dolls growing out of it."

Grandma patted him absently on the head, which made his hat fall over his eyes. "We'll get everything back to the house, and I'm sure you'll be able to do something with the plant."

Lucinda and Evan each took an end of Katie's robot and started to carry it out of the auditorium. Winston followed them out.

Grandma plucked a few Barbies off the plant. "It's a good bloomer. Despite everything, it seems quite healthy in its own way."

Miss Pipkins stood there staring at Katie and me. "I never imagined . . . ," she started to say, before she wandered off into the crowd without finishing her thought.

"What's with her?" Katie asked.

"She's super high-strung. She's going to have to make a million checklists before she feels better," I explained.

"Willow!" I heard a voice call out. I turned around and got whacked in the head with a hard rubber tube about an inch long. It bounced off my head and hit the floor. I picked it up and looked over to see Nathan. "You've got lousy reflexes," he said.

"You can't just call someone's name and expect they will know someone is going to throw something at them," I said. "What is it, anyway?"

"It's the valve from our heart." He picked it up and bounced it on the floor.

Even though Nathan threw something at me I was still grateful he'd helped me out. "Thanks for taking part of the blame for my project."

Nathan smiled. "It's all right. Technically, Bethany and I did cheat. Her dad made the whole project. Besides, I didn't really want to go to space camp."

"You didn't? What happened to being a space smuggler?"

"They don't teach you the fun stuff like that at space camp. You gotta sort it out on your own. Besides, space camp is the same time as my soccer camp." Nathan puffed up his chest. "I was made captain of my team last summer. I'm pretty good."

"I don't know much about soccer," I admitted.

"Given how things go with you, we're probably lucky. The ball would probably explode." Nathan laughed. I laughed too, like I thought it was a joke, but he was probably right. "If you wanted, you could come watch one of my soccer games sometime."

"Me?" My voice sounded a bit squeaky to me.

"I mean, only if you want to. It's no big deal if you don't want to come. Lots of people don't like soccer."

"No! I love soccer. It's my favorite sport." I remembered I had already admitted I didn't know much about soccer. "I mean, what I know about soccer I like."

Nathan didn't seem to notice I was being a spaz. "Cool." He looked at his watch. "I should go, I'm supposed to meet my parents out front." He waved at Katie and me as he headed toward the door.

"So you love soccer, huh?" Katie said with a smile.

I punched her lightly in the arm. "I don't know if I love soccer or not, but I do think it's sort of interesting."

We giggled. There was a squeal from the loudspeaker on the front stage.

"Attention! We have an announcement!" a science fair organizer called out. People stopped packing up their projects and turned to listen. "We just got word that there is an extra trip to space camp for us to give away. We're going to draw a name at random from everyone who participated in the science fair."

The crowd gave an excited murmur. I looked at

Katie, she had all her fingers crossed on both hands. I quickly crossed mine, too. If I could have crossed my toes I would have. I couldn't figure out why they didn't just give the prize to the second place winner, but I was glad they had decided to do it this way so Katie had a chance. The organizer stuck her hand in a giant fishbowl full of white slips. Slowly she pulled a slip out. I bit down on my lip.

"The winner of the extra trip to NASA Space Camp is . . ."

Katie squeezed her eyes shut.

I held my breath.

"KATIE HILLEGONDS!"

Katie leaped so far in the air it looked like she could fly. She bounced up and down. I hugged her and dragged her toward the stage so she could accept the prize.

I stood near the stage while Katie shook hands with the organizer. Miss Pipkins tapped me on the shoulder.

"It's nice to see her get her wish," Miss Pipkins said.

"I didn't do anything," I said, holding my hand up like I was taking a vow.

She laughed. "I know you didn't. I'll be turning in a new report to the Fairy Council. I'm impressed. If humdrums can give up their wishes for us, then maybe fairies do need to know them better."

"She is a pretty special humdrum," I said.

"And you're pretty special too," Miss Pipkins said. She pulled her bag open and reached in for her badge.

"I'm getting my magic back?" I felt almost as excited as Katie had looked when she knew she was going to NASA.

There was a sudden pink light in front of my eyes and a loud *crack* sound. I felt my fingers tingle. "Try to avoid flying out of here or causing any sort of incidents. You're only in Sprite Level 4, there's plenty of time for you to cause more trouble. Don't feel like you have to do all of it in one year," Miss Pipkins said.

I had to fight to keep from floating up. I was so happy. "Yes, ma'am." I bounced up and down on my toes waiting for Katie to get off the stage so I could tell her my news. I accidentally backed into the fishbowl full of names sitting on the edge of the stage, and it fell to the floor, spilling out slips of paper.

I bent down to pick up the paper and stuff them back into the bowl. *Wait a minute. That can't be right.* I looked closely at one slip. Then I picked up another. They were all the same. Every slip of paper had Katie's name on it. I looked up, shocked. Suddenly I knew that it wasn't an accident they had given away another prize.

Miss Pipkins winked. "This one will be our secret. If we can't do a bit of extra magic for those who deserve it, then what's the point of having it? " She smiled one more time and then walked away.

I couldn't believe it. I guess you never know who might grant your wish.

sixteen

Question:

If you have solved your gnome problem, gotten your magic back, had your best friend get her wish granted, *and* managed to do it all without getting into any more trouble, what do you do next?

Answer:

I don't know, but I can't wait to find out.

"I wonder if anyone would notice if I took one of those bones," a voice said behind me. I spun around to see Winston sitting there looking longingly at the giant T. rex skeleton in the lobby.

My heart sped up. I could hear him. Things were back to normal. "No eating dinosaurs," I scolded him with a smile. I'd really missed his furry voice.

Winston jumped up on me, his tail whipping back and forth. "You can hear me again!" I crouched down and rubbed his ears. I was happy too. "We should get a snack to celebrate. Nothing says 'party' like bologna," Winston said.

Lucinda walked up to us. "Do you want a ride home? Evan and Grandma have everything packed into the car."

"I need to wait for Katie," I explained.

"We could stop on the way home and all get some ice cream," Lucinda suggested.

I looked at her with one eyebrow up. "Do you really want Katie and me around?"

Lucinda lightly punched my shoulder. "I guess you're not so bad to have around. For a kid sister, you're pretty cool."

I couldn't believe it. My sister said something nice about me.

"But don't get any ideas. I don't want you around all the time," Lucinda said with a smile.

I wasn't sure about the bologna, but Winston was right, it was time to celebrate.

Find out how it all began!

one

Why having an older sister is a pain:
- She never lets you touch her stuff.
- She bosses you around all the time.
- She acts like she knows *everything*.
- Your parents will let her do all kinds of things that you aren't allowed to do.
- She gets all the new outfits and you have to wear hand-me-downs (even though her favorite color is green, which you hate).

I can think of a lot more reasons, but I would need more paper. Everyone is always surprised to find out Lucinda is my sister. This is because stuff has never spilled on her shirt and her hair never sticks up. She always remembers to say thank you, please, and excuse me. My sister always has her homework done on time, she never snorts when she laughs. Oh, and she can fly.

My sister is a pain.

I lay underneath the hedge in front of my school so I could peek out onto the sidewalk. There was large sign announcing COTTINGLEY FAIRY ACADEMY: TRAINING SPRITES IN THE ART OF FAIRY GODMOTHERING SINCE 1254. Of course the sign was enchanted, so when any humans looked over all they saw was the brass plaque that said COTTINGLEY PRIVATE SCHOOL in front of a small brick building. Our actual school was the size of a castle, but obviously that would stick out, so it was enchanted too.

A group of kids were coming. I hunkered down so they wouldn't see me. It was the same group that walked by every morning on the way to their school. I'd been studying them since the summer. As a fairy-godmother-to-be, I was focused on learning all about humans, or humdrums as we called them, even though I was still only sprite status 2. It was important if I was going to be able to grant wishes someday.

"Willow? What are you doing down there?" My sister wrinkled up her nose. "Your clothes are getting all dirty."

I spun around to glare at her. Why did my sister

have to be so nosy *and* so loud? I motioned for her to be quiet. The girl named Miranda was in the middle of all of her friends. I scribbled down in my notebook what she was wearing.

"Are you spying on them?" Lucinda asked loud enough so they turned around to look as they went by. I scooted out from under the hedge quickly and whacked against the school sign. I stood up, brushing off my shirt. There was a big grass stain on the sleeve.

"I told you you'd get dirty." Lucinda crossed her arms. She was only thirteen, but she acted like she was all grown up. "Why don't you read about humdrums in books like everyone else?"

"I like them; they're interesting."

Another girl wandered by, singing out loud with her music player. She would take a couple steps, stop and do a shimmy dance, and then start walking again. Her outfit had every color in the rainbow. Lucinda looked at me with one eyebrow raised.

"Okay," I admit, "she's a weird one, but those other girls were interesting."

The girl saw us standing by the school gate. She took out her earphones and waved as she walked past. "Hi!"

Lucinda's mouth pressed into a thin line before

giving a stiff wave back. "Great, now the humdrum is paying attention to us."

"This isn't my fault." I hoped I wouldn't get in trouble. Fairies weren't supposed to attract human attention.

"Just like the mud all over your uniform isn't your fault?"

Before I could say anything, my shirt puffed out with a whistle of wind and all the dirt and mud popped off and drifted back to the ground.

I spun around. "Grandma!" She was leaning against the school gate, her silver hair pulled back into a bun.

"We're not supposed to use magic to grant our own wishes," Lucinda said. "It's against the rules. Number 10.4.01A."

"Grandmas are allowed to break rules." Grandma gave me a wink. "Especially when our granddaughters have a big birthday coming up."

Lucinda's mouth pinched shut. She was not a fan of breaking the rules. I also didn't think she's a big fan of fun. I didn't have much when she was around, that's for sure.

"Are you coming to school today?" I asked. My grandma had a full time wish-granting job in the human world as the principal of the humdrum school, but sometimes she would teach a class for us.

"I just stopped by to drop off some cupcakes." Grandma pulled a box tied with pink twine out from behind her back. In glittery letters it said across the top ENCHANTED SUGAR BAKERY.

I clapped my hands together. Enchanted Sugar was the best bakery in town—even the humdrums thought so. My mom owned the bakery and made the best cupcakes in the whole world.

"Her birthday isn't until tomorrow," Lucinda pointed out.

"I think birthday cupcakes belong on Monday, it makes the week sweeter. Besides, I wanted to give you my present early." She pulled a thick silver envelope covered with polka dots from her pocket.

I peeled the flap of the envelope open and slid out a thick piece of white paper. In shiny gold writing it said:

**THIS CERTIFICATE ENTITLES WILLOW THALIA DOYLE
TO ATTEND RIVERSIDE ELEMENTARY SCHOOL
(A HUMDRUM SCHOOL) FOR A PERIOD OF TWO WEEKS.**

My mouth fell open. I threw my arms around Grandma. This was going to be the best birthday ever!

Eileen Cook spent most of her teen years wishing she was someone else or somewhere else, which is great training for a writer. When she was unable to find any job postings for world-famous-author positions, she went to Michigan State University and became a counselor so she could at least support her book-buying habit. But real people have real problems, so she returned to writing. She liked having the ability to control the ending, which is much harder to do when you're a human.

Eileen lives in Vancouver with her husband and dogs and no longer wishes to be anyone or anywhere else. You can read more about Eileen, her books, and the things that strike her as funny at eileencook.com.